Samuel French Acting Edition

I0591834

Saving Grace

by Jack Sharkey

SAMUELFRENCH.COM   SAMUELFRENCH.CO.UK

Copyright © 1976 by Jack Sharkey
All Rights Reserved

SAVING GRACE is fully protected under the copyright laws of the United
States of America, the British Commonwealth, including Canada, and
all other countries of the Copyright Union. All rights, including professional and amateur stage productions, recitation, lecturing, public
reading, motion picture, radio broadcasting, television and the rights of
translation into foreign languages are strictly reserved.

ISBN 978-0-573-61510-8

www.SamuelFrench.com
www.SamuelFrench.co.uk

FOR PRODUCTION ENQUIRIES

UNITED STATES AND CANADA
Info@SamuelFrench.com
1-866-598-8449

UNITED KINGDOM AND EUROPE
Plays@SamuelFrench.co.uk
020-7255-4302

Each title is subject to availability from Samuel French, depending
upon country of performance. Please be aware that *SAVING GRACE* may
not be licensed by Samuel French in your territory. Professional and
amateur producers should contact the nearest Samuel French office or
licensing partner to verify availability.

CAUTION: Professional and amateur producers are hereby warned that
SAVING GRACE is subject to a licensing fee. Publication of this play(s)
does not imply availability for performance. Both amateurs and profes-
sionals considering a production are strongly advised to apply to Samuel
French before starting rehearsals, advertising, or booking a theatre. A
licensing fee must be paid whether the title(s) is presented for charity or
gain and whether or not admission is charged. Professional/Stock licensing fees are quoted upon application to Samuel French.

No one shall make any changes in this title(s) for the purpose of
production. No part of this book may be reproduced, stored in a retrieval
system, or transmitted in any form, by any means, now known or yet to
be invented, including mechanical, electronic, photocopying, recording,
videotaping, or otherwise, without the prior written permission of the
publisher. No one shall upload this title(s), or part of this title(s), to any
social media websites.

For all enquiries regarding motion picture, television, and other media
rights, please contact Samuel French.

Please refer to page 94 for further copyright information.

SAVING GRACE had its world premiere on May 25, 1976, at Limestone Valley Dinner Theatre (Jericho Productions—Joshua F. Cockey, General Manager and Producer), Cockeysville, Maryland, with the following cast:

GRACE LARKIN, a private secretary ..... *Nancy Linehan*

WALTER CHEPPLE, her boss .... *Jon Barry Wilder*

ALEX DOCKER, a telephone repairman .... *Bruce Kaiden*

HARRIET LARKIN, Grace's older sister .. *Spring Condoyan*

GREGOR VANITZKY, a traveling evangelist *Earle Edgerton*

Directed by *Earle Edgerton*
Sound, Lighting by *Judy Hashagen*
Set design by *Tony Mendez*
Costumes by *Jay Scott*
Properties by *D. Lynn Hyman*

TIME: the present

LOCALE: Grace's apartment in Jackson Heights, Long Island, just across the East River from Manhattan

ACT ONE

A late Friday afternoon in mid-January

ACT TWO

Immediately following

ACT THREE

About two hours later

Saving Grace

ACT ONE

Curtain rises on the nominal "apartment" of GRACE
LARKIN *in Jackson Heights, Long Island, a short
drive from Manhattan. It is one of those dreadful
jerrybuilt places with which the Greater New York
area abounds; it was probably a large single bedroom in a former bungalow-style residence, which
now has—by the helterskelter addition of extra
walls and various appurtenances installed wherever
handiest to plumbing, gas fittings and wiring—been
made into a functional but not quite beautiful suite
of rooms. Starting from Downstage Left, we find a
lightswitch on the wall beside the door to the hall.
Just above the door is a hip-high storage cabinet
with a counter top, and a hutch about half the depth
of the cabinet set back against the wall on top of it.
The cabinet contains things like pots and pans, the
hutch contains things like cups and saucers and a
tray of cutlery; at the back of the counter, beneath
the overhang of the hutch, are bottles and jars, rang-
ing in contents from instant coffee through ketchup
to a bottle each of wine and whiskey. Tucked into
the corner above this is a small four-burner range/
oven/broiler with a kettle on the range. Beside this,
against the Upstage wall, is an ancient refrigerator
with the cooling coils on top; a pair of pantyhose
are dangling from the coils down the front of the
refrigerator, apparently to dry. Centered in the Upstage wall beside the refrigerator is a large sash window flanked by pretty curtains; through the window*

—we are on the second floor—we can see some snow on the horizontal parts of the window frame and the second-floor exteriors of bungalows just across the street; it is late afternoon, and as the act progresses, darkness will hide them from view, except for rectangular lights where their windows are. Just Right of the window, tucked into the Upstage Right corner, is a five-foot Christmas tree, modestly decorated and near death from lack of water. Below the tree in the Right wall is an archway masked with colorful bead curtains; this leads to the bedroom and bath. Just below the archway, the wall jogs Right and then down toward Downstage Right again; not fitted too well in this jog are a two-seater sofa which juts out into the room somewhat, a telephone on a small table in the corner, an armchair against the wall below the telephone, and a small coffee table before the armchair. Dead Center Stage is an inexpensive chrome-legged kitchen table, crowded by matching chairs Top, Left and Right. Before the Righthand chair on the table are a coffee cup and saucer, a cereal bowl with a spoon in it, and an open box of Corn Flakes. The room is dim, now, but will flash upon us in all its subdued horror when the light is switched on. However, even though the only salvation for such a room is demolition and rebuilding from scratch, someone has made the place look homey. It is not pretty, but it has been made pretty as possible, and that was no mean task.

*A moment after curtain-rise, we hear running steps in the hall, and then the sound of a key in the lock, and finally—switching on the light as she dashes into the room—*GRACE LARKIN *enters our lives. She is dressed simply but warmly in a cloth coat, woolen muffler and fuzzy beret, and when she removes them she will be seen in a cheery dress suitable for office wear. Right* *now, however, she is very busy. She lurches Upstage and grabs the pantyhose from the refrigerator, flips them serape-fashion across one shoulder, and without pausing rushes down to grab the cereal box off the table and place it on the counter, back beneath the overhang of the hutch, then hastens back to stack and grab up cup, saucer, bowl and spoon and vanish with them through the bead curtains. She is gone for only about three seconds, and then she is back again minus pantyhose and table items. She stands beside the table removing her beret and catching her breath as* WALTER CHEPPLE *appears in the hall doorway. He is pleasant-faced, middle-aged and very well dressed in a fur-collared overcoat and homburg. His expression as he appears is uncertain, but as he recognizes* GRACE *he smiles. It is not an unpleasant smile, and you feel that if he were not twice* GRACE'S *age the two of them would make a very attractive couple.*

WALTER. So this is where you live.

GRACE. (*Still a bit breathless, waves vaguely at room.*) This is it. (*Starts to remove coat.*)

WALTER. (*Steps just inside room.*) I like it.

GRACE. I don't. But come in anyway.

WALTER. (*Steps further inside, leaving door open, sets homburg on table, and is removing overcoat when he notices tree.*) Your tree is very attractive. Decorate it yourself?

GRACE. (*Placing her coat on chair, Right.*) I'm afraid so.

WALTER. (*Dropping own coat on chair, Left.*) No, I really like it. So many nice ornaments.

GRACE. It's only decorated on one side. The part you can't see is bare.

WALTER. Is that why you don't have it in front of the window?

GRACE. Well, no. If I put it there, it'd make the room too dark.

WALTER. (*The small talk is wearing thin.*) Oh, I see.

GRACE. (*Trying to fill the void.*) This table usually goes there. Where the tree is. I had to move the table down here. So I could put the tree there.

WALTER. Why didn't you put the tree here, where the table is?

GRACE. Because of the ornaments. I can only decorate one side with what I have.

WALTER. Oh.

GRACE. I suppose I *could* have put it here, and spread the ornaments out evenly all over it. But it would have looked skimpy.

WALTER. Yes, I guess it would.

GRACE. Besides, I can only look at one side at a time, anyhow. So why not do that side up right?

WALTER. That was very good thinking.

GRACE. (*Very desperate to keep the conversation going.*) Of course, when I get up in the morning, I keep running into the table in the dark. I'm not used to it right here.

WALTER. Why don't you put the light on?

GRACE. (*Pointing.*) Because the switch is over there. I have to cross the room to get to it. So I always bump into the table.

WALTER. That's too bad.

GRACE. I don't mind, really. That's why I put it there.

WALTER. So you could bump into it?

GRACE. No. So I wouldn't bump into the tree. I mean, if the tree was here. Where the table is. I might knock it over.

WALTER. That's true. And break the ornaments. (*They are both out of small talk, now, and stand looking everywhere but at one another for about five seconds; then:*)

GRACE. (*Very quickly.*) Would you like a glass full of whiskey?

WALTER. I beg your pardon?

GRACE. A glass full of whiskey. You know. To drink.

WALTER. Grace, I know what a glass of whiskey is for. It's just—you have such an unusual way of offering it.

GRACE. I—I never had a man up here before. Or anywhere. That's why.

WALTER. That's why what?

GRACE. Why I'm talking so much.

WALTER. You're doing just fine. Uh— (*Glances toward hall, then back to her.*) would you mind if I closed the door?

GRACE. (*In a loud squeak.*) *No!* (*Then, when he hesitates, uncertainly, she clarifies in a hasty babble:*) I mean no-I-don't-mind, not no-don't-close-it. Close it.

WALTER. Are you sure?

GRACE. No. But please close it anyway. (*As soon as he does so:*) Well, that's that!

WALTER. What's what?

GRACE. The worst part. I'm glad it's over with, Mister Chepple.

WALTER. (*Coming back to his side of the table.*) Grace, do you know how silly that sounds?

GRACE. But I'm used to calling you Mister Chepple. Sir.

WALTER. That's in the office. This isn't the office.

GRACE. It certainly isn't. It feels funny. Having you here.

WALTER. Grace, we've known each other for four years.

GRACE. We certainly have. But at the office—it's different. At the office, you're not a man.

WALTER. What?

GRACE. I mean, you don't *act* like a man—! No, wait, that's worse.

WALTER. Grace, I know what you meant to say. At the office there is a certain decorum to be preserved. However, I think you may have noticed that—lately—even there—I've begun to think about you as something more than simply my secretary—?

GRACE. Yes. Yes, I have. And—really—I'm terribly flattered, Mister Chepple.

WALTER. I wish you'd call me Walter. I call you Grace, don't I?

GRACE. Not always. Sometimes you call me Miss Larkin.

WALTER. Okay, I'll make you a deal: Sometimes, *you* call me *Walter*. Fair?

GRACE. I'll certainly try. (*Beat.*) Would you like that whiskey now?

WALTER. Only if you'll join me.

GRACE. Oh, I will. I think it might help to relax me. (*Moves toward counter.*)

WALTER. Me, too. Your nervousness is contagious. (*Conversationally, as she gets bottle and glasses.*) How is it you haven't taken your tree down yet?

GRACE. Oh. Well. I'm never sure how long to leave it up. Most people say till Little Christmas—only I can never remember when it comes.

WALTER. January Sixth. Last week.

GRACE. Oh, dear. I'm sorry. You must think I'm a terrible housekeeper.

WALTER. (*Has strolled to tree, now, and takes hold of a branch.*) Not at all. It certainly brightens up this room. (*Branch comes off in his hand.*) Oops—!

GRACE. (*Turns, sees.*) I also keep forgetting to water it. Just—put that anyplace.

WALTER. (*Tucks it back into position somehow.*) There. You can hardly notice the difference. How's that drink coming?

GRACE. (*Hesitates with open bottle at lip of glass.*) Fine. Only—how much do you want? I mean—I don't know how much men drink.

WALTER. Here, let me. (*Will move to her; takes bottle and glass.*) You get some ice.

GRACE. Oh, yes, of course, ice! (*Will get tray of cubes from refrigerator.*) I don't usually drink whiskey. Sometimes a little bit in my coffee on a cold morning. Mostly I like wine.

WALTER. (*Has poured his drink, pauses before pouring hers.*) Would you rather——?

GRACE. Oh, no. If you have whiskey, I'll have whiskey. I mean, I should join my guest, right? Or isn't that right?

WALTER. Whichever you prefer. Really.

GRACE. Oh. Well, then. I'll have the whiskey. Here's the ice. (*As he finishes fixing both drinks.*) It was very kind of you to drive me home, Mister Chepple. I mean, it's considerably out of your way. You should be home—relaxed—having a good time.

WALTER. (*Hands drink to her, picks up his own.*) What makes you think I'm not having a good time?

GRACE. Oh. That's—very kind of you, Mister Ch— (*Beat.*) Walter.

WALTER. There, you see how easy it is? (*Raises glass.*) Bottoms up! (*Drinks, and after a pause,* GRACE *drains her glass, too.*)

GRACE. (*Blinks a bit at strength of drink, then smiles bravely and hands him her glass.*) Hit me again.

WALTER. (*Reacts; then:*) Where *do* you pick up your idioms?!

GRACE. "I'll Cry Tomorrow."

WALTER. What?

GRACE. "I'll Cry Tomorrow." The movie. Why, did I say it wrong?

WALTER. (*Starts to turn toward bottle with her glass, pauses for:*) Grace—I don't think you understand—there aren't any *rules* to all this. You're only supposed to say what comes into your head, naturally. I mean, I'm not here to score you for accuracy! Now, let's pretend you just handed me that glass. What's the first thing comes into your mind?

GRACE. "Hit me again." (*He pauses, then gives a*

what's-the-use shrug, and pours more whiskey over her remaining ice; she watches; then:) I'm sorry I'm such a klutz, Mister Chepple.

WALTER. Nobody said you were a klutz. (*Turns and hands her fresh drink.*) And the name is Walter. (*She takes drink with hesitant smile; he turns and starts to freshen his own; as he does so:*) This ice cube tray is making a puddle on your counter— (*Glances about, curiously.*) I don't see your sink. Do you have one?

GRACE. It's in the bathroom. Here— (*Will tear a paper towel off a roll on the counter and place it beneath ice cube tray during:*)

WALTER. You mean the bathroom sink? You don't have a kitchen sink?

GRACE. Well—it's both. It's a regular full-sized kitchen sink, but it's in the bathroom, so I guess you could call it the bathroom sink, too. (*Has finished with tray, now faces him uncertainly.*) Why don't we sit down—? Over there, in the living room? (*Gestures toward sofa/armchair area.*) That is, if you have time to sit down.

WALTER. All the time in the world. (*Starts toward sofa.*)

GRACE. (*Babbling as they go, to cover her nervousness.*) It's not really a living room. Nothing in this apartment is really anything. I call it the living room because I'd feel funny having the sofa in the kitchen. Or the stove in the living room, depending on how you look at it. (*They are now side by side before the sofa.*)

WALTER. (*Gallantly, as though they'd entered another room.*) Say, I really like your living room!

GRACE. Oh, *thank* you.

WALTER. (*Clinks glasses with her.*) Cheers.

GRACE. Cheers. (*Both take a small sip; he sighs, satisfied, she makes face.*) The bubbles tickle my nose.

WALTER. What?

GRACE. The bubbles tickle my nose. . . . "Ninotchka."

WALTER. (*Raises glass.*) *Na zdrovie!* (*They drink.*)

GRACE. I guess we may as well sit down. (*They sit; he sits squarely, she sits gingerly, almost on the arm of the sofa, the better to be not too near to him.*) You're a very kind man.

WALTER. What brought that on?

GRACE. You did. I mean—you said there weren't any rules. Just to say the first thing that came into my head. That did, so I said it.

WALTER. Well, I guess that's fair enough. (*Sets glass deliberately on coffee table, shifts to face her; sensing his next move, she clutches her glass with both hands.*) Grace— (*He can't think of a good preliminary, so he abruptly lunges for her, but she just as abruptly surges to her feet, so that he sprawls on sofa behind her; he remains there for:*) You have amazing reflexes, Grace.

GRACE. (*Hasn't moved from spot; stares out front, clutching glass.*) Thank you, Mister Chepple. (*Fishes for return compliment as he straightens back to his original position on sofa; then she finds one:*) And you move very spryly for a man your age.

WALTER. Let's leave my age out of this, okay?! (*Angrily grabs up drink, gulps at it as she sits once more.*)

GRACE. It was supposed to be a compliment. I'm sorry.

WALTER. Okay. (*Sips drink morosely.*)

GRACE. (*Desperate for conversation.*) Would you like to see your Christmas present?

WALTER. You bought me a Christmas present?

GRACE. No, you bought *me* one. Remember?

WALTER. Oh. That. Of course I remember. It took all my courage. And you never said a word about it.

GRACE. I said thank you. I'm sure I did.

WALTER. Only when I handed you the package at the office. Never a word after you got it home and looked at it. I thought you'd say something then!

GRACE. Oh, I did. I said "Wow!"

WALTER. I mean to *me!*

GRACE. I didn't *know* what to say.

WALTER. Didn't you like it?

GRACE. Oh—yes, sure I did.

WALTER. Then why didn't you say so?

GRACE. Because—well—you'd want to *discuss* it, then, and—honestly—I can't imagine what *possessed* you to buy me such a thing! No, wait. I *can* imagine. That's *why* I didn't want to discuss it.

WALTER. All right. We won't discuss it.

GRACE. (*Beat; then:*) Whatever possessed you to buy me such a thing?!

WALTER. (*Edges closer to her, tries man-of-the-world tone.*) Look, Grace—you know our annual sales convention is being held in Hawaii next month—and I've been pulling strings to get permission for you to come along—

GRACE. What would a secretary do at an insurance convention?

WALTER. Uh—oh—take notes at the meetings. That sort of thing.

GRACE. Oh, come *on*, now, Mister Chepple! What would I *do* with the notes? Blackmail the company officers?

WALTER. Grace, we really do discuss business at these conventions! If there's a little—freedom—it's only because our agents have worked hard all year, and need a chance to unwind.

GRACE. Unwind? They fall apart!

WALTER. Grace, you mustn't listen to nasty rumors—

GRACE. I don't have to listen. I've seen the company photographer's photo file—the pictures that *don't* get published in the company magazine!

WALTER. Like what?!

GRACE. Like the Agent of the Year goosing the chairman's mother!

WALTER. That was an accident. Everybody said so. He just happened to be gesturing as she backed up.

GRACE. Three times?

WALTER. So he's accident prone! The point is, those are just fringe benefits—*events!* Most of the time is spent at very important discussions.

GRACE. What do they discuss?

WALTER. Why—um—oh—*lots* of things! Good grief, Grace, you can't expect me to remember every last little detail of a five-day convention!

GRACE. I didn't ask for *every* detail.

WALTER. (*Racks his brain; then:*) You're right! I can't remember even *one.* (*Beat.*) And that's just my point! With you there—at my side—taking notes—

GRACE. I can't. I just can't. I'd be too embarrassed.

WALTER. What *are* you talking about?

GRACE. That *present* you bought me! If you expect me to wear a thing like that—

WALTER. Nonsense! I can see you now, out on the beach, admiring glances flying your way from all sides—

GRACE. But Mister Chepple—

WALTER. Walter.

GRACE. All right: *Walter!* I couldn't appear in public in an outfit like—

WALTER. What public? It'll be all insurance agents!

GRACE. Sure it will! Selling me sunburn protection! (*Stands before he can protest this.*) Look, there's a simple way to settle this: Would you like to *see* the outfit?

WALTER. Grace, I've already *seen* it. I *bought* it.

GRACE. I mean—*on* me?

WALTER. (*Afraid to hope.*) You mean—*now* . . . *here* . . . ?

GRACE. I don't mean at the office!

WALTER. (*Stifling his anticipation so he doesn't scare her off.*) That's right. This—um—*would* be a better place. . . .

GRACE. I'll just be a minute. (*Sets drink on coffee table, starts off, but stops for:*)

WALTER. Grace—what—uh—what happened to your nervousness, all at once?

GRACE. It's—oh—it's just that this is easier than talking to you! I have absolutely no conversation.

WALTER. I thought we were having a *lovely* conversation—?

GRACE. I mean like in the movies. Funny remarks. Brilliant and brittle things. Witty things.

WALTER. (*Sincerely.*) But—honestly, Grace—I thought you were doing just *fine* . . . ?

GRACE. Oh, sure I was! (*With self-mockery:*) "I bump into tables in the dark! . . . I only trim one side of the Christmas tree! . . . How much do men drink?"! (*Grabs up glass, takes deep swallow, emptying it; then:*) I'm a regular Rosalind Russell. (*Hands him her glass.*) Here, make us a couple more while I go and change.

WALTER. (*Very uneasy, and not sure why.*) Grace— are you sure you want to go through with this?

GRACE. No. No, I'm not. (*Moves quickly to point Upstage of sofa before bead curtains.*) It's just—I don't want to end up like Isobel Elsom!

WALTER. *Who?* (*Comes slowly to his feet, drink in hand.*)

GRACE. Isobel Elsom. In the movie, "*Between Two Worlds.*"

WALTER. I didn't see it.

GRACE. (*Accusingly.*) It was *made* in the nineteen-forties . . .

WALTER. (*Resents this return to his age.*) I *still* didn't see it!

GRACE. Well, I did.

WALTER. In the nineteen-forties?!

GRACE. On television.

WALTER. Oh.

GRACE. Well, everybody was on this *boat*—John Garfield, Eleanor Parker, Paul Henreid, Edmund Gwenn—

WALTER. And Isobel Elsom?

GRACE. Of course! That's the whole point!

WALTER. *What* point?!

GRACE. They were all *dead!*

WALTER. Must have been damn little dialogue.

GRACE. No-no! They didn't *know* they were dead. And this boat was taking them from earth to heaven. Or—or *not* to heaven. And Sidney Greenstreet was their judge, and Isobel Elsom had always been the most awful snob, so he sentenced her to move into a beautiful villa or chateau or something.

WALTER. And the non-snobs got to stoke the furnaces—?

GRACE. You don't understand. That was her *punishment*. A beautiful estate, the finest carpets and drapes, gleaming crystal, polished silverware, all kinds of statues and paintings and—

WALTER. *That* kind of punishment *I* could take!

GRACE. But you still don't understand. . . . She was going to be all *alone* there. No one could ever come to see her, for the rest of her eternal life. Don't you see? What's the use of having all those lovely things if you can't show them off to anybody?

WALTER. Ah! Now I see! Ummmph! That *was* pretty horrible. But what's that got to do with—? (*Suddenly gets it.*) Oh!

GRACE. Exactly. What's the point of having something so nice if nobody ever gets to look at it? So I'm going to put your Christmas present on. I have nobody else to put it on *for!*

WALTER. (*Stands and stares at her for a long moment; then:*) I'm going to have another drink. (*Heads right over toward counter, a shaken man.*)

GRACE. Are you—upset?

WALTER. (*Lifts bottle without facing her, hesitates short of pouring.*) I don't know *what* I am. (*Starts to pour, stops again.*) All I meant—I just thought it would be nice, driving you home—you and me, here alone together—and now— (*Beat.*) I don't know *what* I am! (*Pours a stiff one and drinks it down.*)

GRACE. I'll be back in a minute . . .

WALTER. (*Still without turning.*) I'll *be* here. (*Satisfied, she exits through bead curtains; alone, he hesitates, then pours himself a moderate drink, turns and glances toward curtains, comes to a decision, calls.*) Do you mind if I use your phone?

GRACE. (*Off.*) Oh, no. Help yourself. It's right there in the corner by the sofa.

WALTER. (*Crossing toward phone.*) It's just—these friends of mine— I thought I was going to stop by at their place after work—but now—what with you and—uh—everything— (*Stops just before entering sofa area, shakes head as if just a bit dazed, takes a swallow of his drink; then:*) I'd better tell them I've been delayed.

GRACE. (*Off.*) *Oh!*

WALTER. What's the matter—?!

GRACE. (*Comes running out to him, shoeless, but otherwise dressed.*) I forgot. My telephone isn't working. I called from the office today and they said they'd send a man out.

WALTER. On a night like this? Don't you believe it. It must be thirty below zero outside.

GRACE. But they *promised.* . . .

WALTER. Well, don't worry about it. It wasn't an *official* get-together or anything. I just said I *might* drop by. For a drink.

GRACE. For your birthday! How could I forget?! To-day's your birthday! I even put a card on your desk this morning! Your friends are throwing you a birthday party, and you're not going, just because I was going to put on that silly—!

WALTER. Don't be ridiculous. I said I might drop by for a drink after work. And I still might. So go, put that thing on and let's get it over with.

GRACE. Let's get *what* over with?

WALTER. Will you stop being so nervous?!

GRACE. I can't help it. You know why. I'm a woman—

WALTER. You sure are.

GRACE. And you're a man—

WALTER. I'm glad you noticed.

GRACE. And, oh, it's your birthday, and this is such a lonesome apartment to be in, and I still have a little Christmas spirit left, and—

WALTER. And what?

GRACE. Would you like to sing carols?

WALTER. Oh, for pete's sake! Hold this. (*Hands her his drink; she takes it; then he takes her by both shoulders and kisses her once, briefly and gently.*) There. Now that wasn't so bad, was it?

GRACE. No. It was very pleasant. That's just the trouble. (*Hands his drink back to him.*) If I wasn't sure kissing you would be pleasant I wouldn't be so nervous!

WALTER. Look, we're both adults—

GRACE. No, we're not. *You're* an adult.

WALTER. (*Stung, draws back.*) What is this *obsession* you have about my *age?!* I'll be forty-three on my next birthday!

GRACE. That's today.

WALTER. Okay-okay! I'm forty-three! I'm not exactly ready for Medicare!

GRACE. (*Shrugs the topic away.*) Nobody is. Well— I guess—I'd better be—uh— (*She is wavering on the brink of exiting through curtains.*) Listen. About your gift. The only reason I'm putting it on—

WALTER. I know, I know. So you won't wind up like Isobel Elsom.

GRACE. Well, yes, *that,* of course—but—I want you to know—I—I don't mean anything *else* by wearing it, if you know what I mean . . . ? I've seen too many movies where the girl only means to get into something comfortable, but the man thinks—

WALTER. (*Beginning to despair of getting her to change.*) Grace, please—! (*Stops, his face lighting up with inspiration; then:*) Movies! Of course! Grace . . . how would you like to be in pictures—?

GRACE. (*Very dubious and negative.*) The kind they show at insurance conventions—?!

WALTER. Of course not! I mean home-movies, with that outfit on you. I have a new *Super-8* camera in the trunk of my car, and—and—um— (*Pauses, his mind working feverishly; then:*) You could play a scene from an old Dorothy Lamour movie!

GRACE. (*Intrigued and excited.*) Which *scene?!*

WALTER. (*Has no idea, and his exasperation shows.*) How the hell should *I* know? *You're* the old-movie expert! Can't *you* think of one?!

GRACE. (*Pondering.*) Uh. Well. How about the one where—Jon Hall comes home, and she jumps into the *volcano!* But the angry natives—

WALTER. (*Interrupts in fury of frustration.*) That's perfect! Now, come on, you get into the outfit, while I hurry down and get the camera, and— (*He is gently turning her by the shoulders to face the bead curtains and trying to force her through them, but she balks.*)

GRACE. Do you think it'll be all right—movies, at this time of night? I mean, with Mrs. Benjamin right downstairs, and that nice young couple in the basement just had a baby, and—

WALTER. Grace, I am bringing up one tiny little hand-held camera, not a twelve-man *sound-crew* in hobnailed *boots!*

GRACE. I thought sound-crew men had to wear crepe soles on their shoes . . . ?

WALTER. Grace—please— Go, don't go, change, don't change—just do *something*, before I go out of my mind!

GRACE. (*Sorry she's upsetting him, nods, exits through curtains on:*) Oh, all right. I'll be back in a jiffy!

WALTER. (*Mutters morosely.*) Probably a floor-length jiffy with a steel belt!

(*There is a KNOCK at the door; he reacts, and—glancing toward the bedroom—he signifies that he is not particularly keen on callers at this moment. So he stands there, not touching the knob, and after a moment he puts his ear to the door and listens. The KNOCK repeats loudly, and he recoils. Then, with resignation and a facade of aplomb, he opens the door and* ALEX DOCKER *steps inside.* ALEX *is about thirty years old, a head taller than* WALTER, *and generally better-looking. His garb is casual—corduroy work pants, a flannel shirt and an unzipped pile-lined winter jacket. He carries a kit of telephone-repair tools in his left hand, and a pair of heavy slip-on workboots with crepe soles. He smiles.*)

ALEX. Telephone company. You reported trouble with your phone?

WALTER. I don't believe it. You came out on a night like this?

ALEX. Phone trouble is phone trouble. Why not?

WALTER. Well—it's after working hours—well past five o'clock.

ALEX. People make a lot of phone calls after work. If the phone isn't working we don't make any money. So here I am.

WALTER. I—I suppose you have some sort of identification?

ALEX. (*Annoyed at this strange reluctance, makes no move to produce any identification, but says:*) Yes, I have.

WALTER. (*After a five-second eyeball-to-eyeball confrontation, wilts.*) Well. That's good. A person can't be too careful. The—uh—the telephone's over there.

ALEX. (*Cheerfully.*) Thanks. (*Goes directly to phone while* WALTER *resignedly shuts door.*) How long has it been on the fritz?

WALTER. Why—um—I don't *know* . . . (*When* ALEX *looks his way, curious:*) See, I don't live here.

ALEX. Oh? (*Takes piece of paper from pocket, consults it.*) Then you're not "G. Larkin?"

WALTER. No. I'm Walter Chepple. I'm Miss Larkin's employer. And friend. (*Importantly produces business card.*) My card.

ALEX. (*Reads card; then:*) What's a D.S.M.?

WALTER. District Sales Manager. I work out of our Manhattan office on the upper East Side.

ALEX. Funny, you don't *look* like a mop salesman . . .

WALTER. Who said I *was?*

ALEX. (*Indicates card.*) It says "MOP." M—O—P.

WALTER. That's "Mutual of Pittsburgh!" (*Snatches card back and repockets it.*) You must have heard of it. The insurance company? Our ads are on TV all the time —the Friendly Fingers of Mutual?

ALEX. (*Turning back to phone.*) I never watch television. Too many other things to do. (*Stands there, smiling conversationally.*)

WALTER. (*With very nervous glance toward bedroom.*) Look, how about getting on with the repairs?!

ALEX. (*Senses the man doesn't want to chat.*) Oh. Sure. (*Lifts phone, listens, hangs up.*) Dead. (*Misses Walter's of-course-it's-dead! facial reaction, sits on sofa, pulls off shoes, starts donning boots.*) It's probably the terminals. Pretty stormy this past week. Something may have blown loose.

WALTER. Can't you hurry it up a little?

ALEX. (*Pauses.*) What's the big rush?

WALTER. (*Another unhappy glance toward bedroom; then:*) Oh—nothing. Nothing at all. Go ahead. What do you have to do?

ALEX. (*Will finish donning boots and stand up during:*) Well, the pole's out front, the input lines are hooked to the outside wall just above the front porch roof, so I'll have to go out there and check the terminals.

That's what the boots are for. Slippery out there. But—
if it's what I think it is, it won't take long. (*Picks up
kit, starts toward window, then stops and turns for:*) Say,
you don't drive a dark blue Chevy, do you?

WALTER. Why—yes. I do. Why do you ask?

ALEX. You left your headlights on. I would've turned
them off, but your car was locked up tighter'n a drum.
(*Slides window open, climbs outside.*) This cold weather's
hard enough on batteries without a slow drain like that.
Better get 'em off quick! (*Edges out of sight toward
Right, vanishes during:*)

WALTER. (*Grabbing up overcoat and homburg.*)
Thanks, I will! Something I had to get out of the trunk,
anyhow . . . ! (*He exits to hall, shuts door behind him;
through the slightly open window, we hear a clanking of
tools, then a hacking sound, then a high-volume-but-brief
splash and gush of water, and:*)

ALEX. (*Off.*) Aaaaah, damn it all!

(*After this outburst, there is a moment more of clanking
and hacking, then silence; then, after a moment, we
hear:*)

GRACE. (*Off.*) Mister Chepple—? . . . Walter—? . . .
Uh—ready or not—here I come! (GRACE *enters through
curtains: She is garbed entirely in* WALTER'S *Christmas
gift—a Hawaiian maiden outfit; it has six parts: a plastic
hibiscus flower behind her ear, a plastic lei about her
neck, a floral-print halter, a grass skirt, and two grass
anklets. She looks simultaneously ravishing and silly.*)
Now, I ask you, why would I wear these plastic flowers
in—? (*Stops as she rounds end of sofa and sees no one;
looks about.*) Walter? . . . Where *are* you—? (*PHONE
rings and she jumps, then answers it.*) Hello? . . . Oh,
hi, Estelle, you startled me. I didn't think my telephone
was working, and when it rang— (*Pauses in puzzlement,
picks up* ALEX'S *shoes by backs in one hand.*) If that

isn't the strangest—! . . . What? Oh. Well, Mister
Chepple was here a moment ago, but he seems to have
left—except that he forgot his *shoes*—! . . . Estelle,
don't be silly! . . . Of *course* he had them on the last
time I saw him. . . . He had *everything* on! . . . Oh,
now, *really*, Estelle! (*Hangs up angrily; fumes a moment, then shrugs, starts around end of sofa—and stops
in shock as* ALEX *appears, clambering in window, his
back to her; she goggles, then drops shoes onto sofa,
vanishes through curtains.* ALEX *shuts window and locks
it, turns around, and we see that he is soaking wet;
shivering, he hurries down to phone, sets kit on coffee
table, dials phone.*)

ALEX. . . . Hello, Marge—? . . . Alex Docker . . .
Yeah, it was the terminals. All iced over, and the pres-
sure cracked the insulator and shorted the line. . . . Just
chipped off the ice and replaced the cap. Except that I
also unclogged the bottom of a frozen drainspout and got
about five gallons of ice water all over me. . . . Naw, I'll
survive. . . (GRACE *emerges through curtains, warily,
carrying a huge pistol.*) Oh, yeah, she's in great shape,
now. All warmed up and ready for action. (GRACE *reacts
—pleased at compliment, but uneasy about the source.*)
It's scary on the porch roof, though. Next time I come
here, I think I'll just lean through the bedroom window
and tap her with a hammer. (GRACE'S *hand goes fearfully
to the top of her head.*) No, this was one of my easiest
jobs. I'll just clean up and take off. (GRACE *straightens,
steely-eyed, comes around end of sofa and up in back of*
ALEX, *holding the pistol with two hands, now, and
pointed right at the back of his head.*) Well, what the
hell, it's a living! . . . Yeah. 'Bye, now. (*He hangs up
phone, brushes futilely at front of jacket and shirt, then
flicks water off his hands; without turning, he lifts one
leg—balancing with a slight wobble—and begins the
strugglesome task of pulling off one of his workboots, but
freezes in place, very surprised, on:*)

GRACE. (*A terrified squeak.*) Don't move a muscle or I'll blow your head off!

ALEX. Huh—? (*Still balancing on one foot, starts to turn his head.*) Hey, listen—

GRACE. Stand where you are! (*Started, he wobbles even more, losing his balance.*) I mean it! Don't move or I'll shoot!

ALEX. Lady, have a heart! What the hell do you think I am, a stork?!

GRACE. (*Realizing his problem.*) Oh. Well—all right, put your foot down . . . but don't make any sudden moves!

ALEX. (*Gratefully gets foot back on floor, straightens.*) Can I turn around now?

GRACE. (*Looks quickly down at herself, then at his back again.*) No! Don't move an inch, do you hear me?! Stay just where you are! I'm going to phone the police!

ALEX. It's going to get mighty crowded over here.

GRACE. (*Realizes, as he has, that the phone is beyond where he stands.*) Oh. Yes, I see what you mean. All right, then. Turn around—*very slowly*—but put your hands up and keep them up! Understand?

ALEX. Perfectly. (*Raises hands, then slowly turns around, sees her and reacts.*) Wow! (*Hands waver.*)

GRACE. (*Thrusts pistol forward, and his hands re-elevate, on:*) Keep those hands up!

ALEX. They're up, they're up! Now if you'll just let me explain—

GRACE. You can do your explaining down at the station!

ALEX. You know, I didn't know people said things like that, except in the movies.

GRACE. That's where *I* learned it.

ALEX. You see a lot of movies?

GRACE. Enough, I guess. What's it *to* ya?!

ALEX. For pete's sake, will you stop talking like a Bogart film festival? Let me explain why I'm here—

GRACE. There's no need. I know why. I saw you creeping in through my window!

ALEX. I did not creep! I clambered! It's slippery out there!

GRACE. Scrambling around on porch roofs at your age! You might have got hurt!

ALEX. And that would bother you—?

GRACE. Of *course* it would! I hate to see *anything* get hurt.

ALEX. What do you think *that* is likely to do to me?!

GRACE. Watch it, Mister—this gun is very heavy.

ALEX. Then why don't you put it down?

GRACE. How dumb do you think I am?

ALEX. Well, considering the way you're dressed for Mister Chepple—

GRACE. Mister Chepple—?!

ALEX. You know—the guy with the friendly fingers?

GRACE. So *that's* why he's not here! What have you done with Mister Chepple?!

ALEX. Somehow, I feel *I* should be asking *you* that question. Do employees always dress like this for the district sales manager?

GRACE. The way I dress for Mister Chepple is *my* affair . . . ! I mean, it's my *business* . . . / I mean it's none of *your* business! Now kindly stand away from that telephone! (*Jumps as there is a KNOCK at the door.*)

(*NOTE: Business in following is thus:* GRACE *points pistol at door each time* WALTER *speaks, and* ALEX's *hands come down—then points it at* ALEX *when she speaks to* him, *and his hands go back* up, *etc.*)

WALTER. (*Off.*) Grace?

ALEX. It's the mop salesman.

GRACE. The what?

ALEX. "Mutual of Pittsburgh." Didn't Mister Chepple tell you where you worked?

GRACE. Say, how do you know so much about— Oh!
You were eavesdropping at my window! Oh, dear! How
much did you hear?

ALEX. Why, did I miss something juicy?! (*KNOCK
repeats, more loudly.*)

WALTER. (*Off.*) Grace? Open this door!

ALEX. He sounds anxious.

GRACE. For your information, this is the very first
time I've ever had Mister Chepple in my apartment!

ALEX. And you're dressed like *that?*

GRACE. It's not what you think. This is Mister
Chepple's Christmas present!

ALEX. He wouldn't settle for cigars?

WALTER. (*Off.*) Grace? (*Much louder KNOCKS.*)
Grace, are you all right?

GRACE. Just a minute! (*Turns back just in time to catch
ALEX lowering his hands, shouts:*) Will *you* put your
hands where I *tell* you?

WALTER. (*Off.*) Well— I'll do my *best* . . . *?!*

GRACE. (*Turns head for:*) Not *you!* (*Whirls back, but
this time ALEX hasn't moved an inch.*)

WALTER. (*Off.*) Then *who?!*

GRACE. (*Without turning.*) Nobody! (*A hoarse whisper, to ALEX.*) You! Pick up your burglar tools and get
out of here the way you came in!

ALEX. You're letting me escape?

GRACE. What else can I do?! I don't want Mister
Chepple to find me here this way with a strange man,
and if I call the police I'd have to go down to the station
and swear out a complaint, and it's nearly thirty below
zero outside, and you're soaking wet, and, well—

WALTER. (*Off.*) Grace, who are you talking to?!

GRACE. Nobody! I'm on the telephone!

WALTER. (*Off.*) On the telephone with nobody?

GRACE. (*To ALEX, desperately.*) Will you please get
out of here?!

WALTER. (*Off.*) Grace!

GRACE. I *said* I was on the *telephone!*

WALTER. (*Off.*) Can't you get *off* the telephone a minute and open this *door—?!*

GRACE. I can't! It's a very important call! (*The PHONE rings.*) Oh, dear!

WALTER. (*Off.*) What was *that—?!*

GRACE. (*Lurches forward toward phone, which* ALEX *gallantly grabs up before it can ring again, shouting as she lurches:*) My alarm clock! (*In confusion, she twirls round as she takes phone, ends up with the receiver pressed to* ALEX'S *chest and the muzzle of the gun pressed to her ear, as she shouts:*) Hello—? Hello—?! (ALEX, *his hands down now, gently taps her on shoulder, takes pistol from her and places her hand with receiver in it against her ear; she smiles gratefully, goes to speak on phone, then realizes that this man now holds her pistol, and gapes in horror.*) Oh!

WALTER. (*Off.*) Grace, what's the matter?

ALEX. (*Patiently gestures with gun at phone.*) Your party is waiting.

GRACE. (*Her voice squeaky with fear, manages to speak into phone.*) H-hello—? (*Then, fear giving way before surprise:*) Harriet? . . . Harriet, it *is* you! . . . (*Covers mouthpiece, does an unthinking "aside" to* ALEX.) It's my sister Harriet, all the way from Chillicothe, Ohio! (*As* ALEX *nods in pleasant comprehension, she returns to phone.*) You're where? . . . Oh, my gosh, you can't be! That's only about fifteen minutes away from here! . . . What? . . . (*Looks nervously at* ALEX, *at pistol he holds, then turns her back slightly to him, half-whispering into phone; while she is not looking,* ALEX *breaks pistol open to check if it's loaded, lifts out roll of caps, rolls his eyes in relief, then puts caps into pocket and re-closes pistol.*) Listen, I don't know how to explain this, but— well—you'd better not come over here just now. . . . No, there's nothing wrong, nothing at all. . . . Yes, I know you've come all the way from Chillicothe. . . . I

do *not* sound nervous! . . . Well, *I* ought to know how
I sound, Harriet! . . . Oh, but honestly, it'd be so much
simpler if you just went to a hotel tonight, and then, in
the morning—that is, if I'm still *here* in the morning—?
(*Looks a fearful question at* ALEX, *who smiles warmly
and nods his head, indicating her eventual safety, and
she goes back onto the phone in great relief.*) Yes, it's
okay for tomorrow morning. . . . But Harriet, really—!
No, I'm fine, just fine. . . . Yes, tomorrow. . . . Thank
you. . . . See you then. (*Hangs up, sighing with relief,
then turns angrily to* ALEX.) All the way from Ohio, and
I can't have her over because you're holding me hostage!

(*As they talk, we see* WALTER *again: He is outside the
window, having edged into view from the Left, but
he cannot get the window open, nor see the two of
them thanks to the jut of the wall just above the
telephone table; after a moment's futile pushing at
underside of lower sash, he sidles Off toward Right.*)

ALEX. Look, I'll just check the place out and you can
call her back.

GRACE. But what'll I say? I can't invite her over while
you're casing the joint! How would that look?!

ALEX. How would it look if she found Walter here,
with you in your siren suit?

GRACE. This is *Walter's* siren suit!

ALEX. Really? Maybe I was worrying over nothing!
Here—! (*Returns pistol to her.*)

GRACE. (*Barely realizes she has pistol back, busy
countering his innuendo.*) I mean he *gave* me this outfit
for a *Christmas present!* (*Angrily strides past him, im-
periously points to hall door.*) Now will you please pack
up your burglar tools and go?!

ALEX. What do we tell Walter when you open the
door?

GRACE. Oh. That's right. Okay, then, use the window, but just *go!*

ALEX. How do I get off the porch roof?

GRACE. How did you get *onto* it?!

ALEX. Well, actually— (*Sneezes.*)

GRACE. Oh, dear, I forgot, you're soaking wet! You can't go out like that, you'll freeze solid! Here, take those things off and I'll dry them in the oven! (*Carefully edges around upper end of table, pistol-gesturing him to move around lower end, so he can move up to oven without coming near her, during:*)

ALEX. (*Will get up near oven and remove jacket and shirt.*) Listen, this is all very kind of you, but what if somebody comes in before my things are dry?

GRACE. Oh! Well—I—I'll say you showed up at my door undressed! (*Is watching her imaginary scene on a mind's-eye movie screen, raptly lost in her own story creation.*) You were dazed! . . . You got a blow on the head and lost your memory—that way I won't have to mention your name—by the way, what *is* your name?

ALEX. Alex. Alex Docker. But listen, Miss Larkin—

GRACE. Oh, please call me Grace.

ALEX. Really?

GRACE. Well, I know it's informal on short acquaintance, but if you're going to be standing around in your underwear, formality would be silly!

ALEX. (*With reluctant logic.*) I must admit—you have a point! But this loss-of-memory thing—

GRACE. It'll work, you'll see! Just like Nancy Guild and John Hodiak in *"Somewhere in the Night!"* He didn't know who he was, but she took him in, hiding him from the men who beat him up, and—

ALEX. (*Genuinely impressed.*) Say, you *do* see a lot of movies! (*Sneezes.*) What's your favorite kind?

GRACE. (*Impatient with all this chat and concerned about the sneeze.*) Will you please take your clothes off?!

ALEX. I guess *that* answers my question! (*Starts to*

undo trousers, then straightens.) Wait a minute! *I* can't undress in front of a *customer—!*

GRACE. (*Enthralled by this fascinating criminal.*) Is *that* what you call your victims?

ALEX. Oh! Well—uh—yes, it is. After all, I'm performing a service, and— It's kind of fun!

GRACE. Looting people's homes?!

ALEX. Hell, you're *insured*, aren't you? In your job, you *must* be! Everybody comes out ahead—I get your possessions, you get a nice bundle of money, and buy yourself even *better* possessions!

GRACE. That's the most crooked thing I've ever heard!

ALEX. You mean you *won't* try to collect?

GRACE. Well, of *course* I will! There's nothing wrong with *that—!* I mean, it's not as though I were taking *payola* or anything—!

ALEX. Did it ever occur to you that your business is really just a form of legalized gambling?

GRACE. That's a *terrible* thing to say!

ALEX. What do you mean? You put down your money with the company, and they bet you that you're not going to be robbed—or have a car accident—or drop dead—

GRACE. It's not the same thing at all! There's a world of difference between gambling and insuring!

ALEX. How do you figure? Your statisticians figure out the odds of something happening to you, then you place your bet that it won't, and if it does, they pay off. Right?

GRACE. (*More focused on his bare chest than the conversation.*) Uh—now wait a minute—there's a very great difference between—I mean, after all, everybody *knows* that gambling is—while insurance, on the other hand, is— (*Pauses, thinks, then stares at him, and murmurs huskily:*) You *know* something, I think you're absolutely right—?! (*Absently sets pistol down on table.*)

ALEX. Of course I'm right. A girl of your obvious intelligence should have figured it out for herself.

GRACE. Now look, just because I'm not turning you in

to the police, you needn't feel obliged to lavish me with empty flattery and— (*It hits her.*) *What* did you just call me?

ALEX. (*Blank.*) Intelligent. Is there some reason I shouldn't?

GRACE. (*Almost in delirious shock, says huskily:*) How did you find out?

ALEX. The minute I entered this room and saw there was no television set. (*She reacts uneasily.*) I knew you had to be the brainy sort. I never watch, either. Sell, sell, sell, commercial after commercial—! *Brrr!* (*Gives esthetic shudder, which she misinterprets.*)

GRACE. You've got to get those pants off!

ALEX. (*Hesitates, looks down at himself, then looks at her, then shrugs.*) Why not! (*Will divest himself of pants, and she will put pants, shirt and jacket into oven, over next few lines.*)

GRACE. (*Very embarrassed.*) There! I knew you'd overcome your initial embarrassment. After all, we're both mature, intelligent adults. Both of us. It might *look* a little strange, but as long as we know the *real* reason you're undressed— (*Has pants and things, now.*) Why— they're almost dry. You must be very—hotblooded—! (*Covers her confusion by hastily putting things into oven.*)

ALEX. That reminds me—what's become of the friendly fingers at our door?

GRACE. *Walter!* I forgot all about him! (*Rushes to door, yanks it open, steps out, re-enters after a second looking puzzled, leaving door slightly ajar.*) He's not there . . . ?!

ALEX. He's missing a beautiful sight!

GRACE. He certainly is!

ALEX. I mean *you!* Tell me, Miss Larkin—Grace—do you always dress for the tropics when friends come to call?

GRACE. (*Lying so badly he doesn't accept a word of*

it.) Of course not! This isn't a dress—this is a—um—nightgown! I was just getting ready for bed when Walter dropped in unexpectedly, and—well—I let him in without thinking!

ALEX. Now, *that* part I believe! No woman with a brain like yours would let in a man like that if she'd had a moment to think about it!

GRACE. Will you stop about my brain? You're getting me all mixed up! Maybe it's lucky he's gone. Now *you* can go, and use the stairs instead of the window!

ALEX. I can't go out like *this!*

GRACE. I mean when your clothes are dry.

ALEX. Even then—for some strange reason, I don't like the thought of leaving you here alone.

GRACE. I'm used to being alone.

ALEX. A lovely girl like you?

GRACE. (*Appreciates this, but petulantly turns her back.*) I wish you wouldn't talk that way in your underwear. Besides, I won't be alone. Walter will be back.

ALEX. Is that what you want?

GRACE. I don't know. It's been four years—four years of making excuses, fending him off at the water cooler, pretending I didn't see the way he looked at me, avoiding overtime, ducking out at five o'clock—! (*Beat.*) I just got tired of fighting. . . . (*Turns away quickly, trying not to cry.*)

ALEX. Look. Miss Larkin. I know this is none of my business—

GRACE. (*Faces him, angry.*) You're right! It isn't! Now will you please pack up and go?

ALEX. Does the oven *ding* when my clothes are done?

GRACE. Oh, for heaven's sake, take them! They weren't all *that* wet!

ALEX. (*Almost goes to oven, but turns back.*) Hey. I'll make you a deal. You get your own clothes on, and I'll get mine on and clear out without another word.

GRACE. But—what'll I tell Walter when he comes back?

ALEX. Tell him the "nightgown" was too large, or the wrong color, anything at all!

GRACE. But—

ALEX. I'm not moving from this spot till you make yourself respectable!

GRACE. You said I *was* respectable!

ALEX. I said you were intelligent! I never said a word about respectability.

GRACE. (*Starts reluctantly for bedroom.*) Men! You're all alike!

ALEX. What are you talking about? Walter wants you *in* the nightgown, I want you *out* of it!

GRACE. I mean you're all so damned *bossy!* (*Will exit through curtains during:*) Do this, do that, come here, go there—! (ALEX *has barely had time to shake his head in amusement when all at once we hear running footsteps, and* GRACE *comes bolting back through curtains and right into his arms, her eyes wide with fright, as she gasps in a hoarse whisper:*) There's someone climbing in my bedroom window!

ALEX. Maybe it's another burglar. Tell me—what have *I* got *he* hasn't got?

GRACE. Oh, please don't joke! I'm serious! Do you have a gun?

ALEX. (*Enjoying and maintaining their embrace.*) What's wrong with yours? (*Nods toward table; she looks, then shakes her head.*)

GRACE. *He* might have a *real* one! (*Then she screws up her face in chagrin, realizing she's given away her helplessness and stupidity.*) Oh boy!

(*Before he can reply, there is a CRASH in the bedroom; suddenly startled and alert,* ALEX *thrusts her gently from his arms, rushes to lightswitch and douses all the lights; thanks to the spill from the hall through*

*the slightly-ajar door, and the bit of lighting from
the window, we can still see their forms dimly as he
hurries to his kit, removes a hefty wrench, then takes
a stance, wrench upraised to strike, just Upstage of
the bead curtains; until further notice, he and she
will speak in loud whispers:*)

ALEX. Are you all right?

GRACE. Yes! . . . No!

ALEX. What's the matter?

GRACE. I'm afraid of the dark!

ALEX. (*Looks her way, realizes hall door is still ajar.*)
Well, it's about to get *worse!* Shut that door! He'll see us!
(*Moaning slightly, she nonetheless obediently shuts door,
and room gets considerably darker, though we can still
see the two of them;* ALEX *beckons quickly to her.*) Come
on over here, and stand behind me!

GRACE. What for?

ALEX. He may come out shooting!

GRACE. Ooooooh! (*Races fearfully across room, jumps
behind him and encircles him with her arms, effectively
pinioning his own.*)

ALEX. (*Quietly.*) Grace. I can't move my arms.

GRACE. (*Truly unaware.*) Why not?

ALEX. (*Patiently.*) Because you've pinned them to my
sides.

GRACE. Oh! (*Releases him, and just then there is a
KNOCK at the door.*) It's Walter! He must have come
back!

ALEX. Well, go and let him in!

GRACE. (*Starts for door, but stops after two steps,
turns to him for:*) I thought you didn't like Walter.

ALEX. I don't, but your prowler might be too big for
one man to handle alone!

GRACE. But—two against one isn't fair!

ALEX. Never mind, *I'll* let Walter in! (*Strides past her
across room to door, flings door open, and at that same*

moment WALTER *stumbles in through bead curtains, carrying his movie camera, still in homburg and overcoat, and a terrified* GRACE *sees him and reacts with a shriek:*)

GRACE. He's *here!* (*From here on, of course,* ALEX *and* GRACE *abandon the hoarse whispering they've maintained since she rushed into room.*)

ALEX. *Where—?!*

(*Flips on light, and takes first step of a run toward her, but pulls up short as he sees* WALTER; *at exactly the same time,* GRACE *has run to* ALEX *and leaped up into his arms for protection, not seeing identity of* WALTER *in dark; and just as she embraces him,* HARRIET LARKIN, GRACE'S *older sister, in a cloth coat, thick glasses and unbecoming hairdo, carrying a suitcase, enters from hall; she stops and stares in shock at the same tableau we see: An exotically garbed young girl in the arms of a nearly undressed man, while another man is apparently shooting a film of whatever they are doing. It looks bad, very bad, indeed, and in a quick series of glances at one another,* WALTER, ALEX *and* GRACE *realize just how bad it looks—and then* GRACE *belatedly realizes who it is that just came through the curtains, and does a double-take at him, staring in surprise, on:*)

GRACE. Walter!

HARRIET. (*Trying to formulate a coherent query.*) Grace—?!

GRACE. (*Her tone pleading for understanding.*) Harriet—

ALEX. (*May as well get into the act.*) And my name is Alex.

HARRIET. (*Still in shock, babbles while gesturing with her free hand.*) Grace . . . your outfit . . . that camera . . . and this man has no trousers on . . . ! (*There is a moment of silence; then:*)

GRACE. (*It is both a greeting and an explanation.*)
Welcome to New York.

(*And as* WALTER, ALEX *and* GRACE *attempt sickly smiles
at her, and an open-mouthed* HARRIET *drops her
suitcase with a crash—*)

THE CURTAIN FALLS

ACT TWO

At curtain-rise, everybody is right where we just left them a short intermission ago. They stand staring—HAR-RIET at the guilty trio, the trio at HARRIET—for a frozen moment. And then GRACE, still up in ALEX's arms, speaks as if the terrible tableau had not occurred.

GRACE. Harriet, you must be simply exhausted! Why don't you go right to bed— (ALEX *sets her on her feet.*) —have a lovely sleep, and then in the morning you and I will have a nice cozy chat?!

(Spurred by her commonplace attitude into acting with similarly hopeless geniality, ALEX and WALTER also move—ALEX to close the apartment door, WALTER to hastily drop the incriminating camera onto the sofa—over the following hearty speech:)

ALEX. Splendid idea! It's a long way from Chillicothe to Jackson Heights! What you need is a good night's rest! So, just let me get my clothes out of the oven, and— (*Has taken a pace Upstage toward oven, but stops on:*)

HARRIET. Why is that man's clothing in your oven, Grace?

WALTER. That's what *I'd* like to know!

HARRIET. You mean you don't know, either?

WALTER. Of course not! (*Realizes this needs further explanation, also realizes he has none that will make sense, so he essays valiantly:*) I mean—you see—I'm just a friend. Passing through. They never tell me anything.

GRACE. Harriet, *I* can explain— This whole thing is really *marvelously* innocent—! (*Laughs hollowly.*)

WALTER. It *is?* Uh—I mean it *is!* All innocent, open and aboveboard! (*Then, uncertainly, to* GRACE:) *Isn't* it—?

GRACE. Of course it is!

HARRIET. Oh, I *do* wish I could *believe* that!

WALTER. Oh, you *can!*

HARRIET. Then explain it.

WALTER. (*Passing the hot potato.*) Go ahead, Grace.

GRACE. Harriet—look at it this way—don't you trust your own sister?

HARRIET. In that outfit? Oh, Grace, what would *Mother* say!

GRACE. Nothing. Mother would have fainted a long time ago.

ALEX. Now, Grace, it's not as bad as all *that!*

HARRIET. How bad *is* it?

WALTER. It's not bad at all!

HARRIET. How do you mean that?

GRACE. Look, I'm very simple—I mean, *it* is—I mean —oh, *why* didn't you go to a *hotel?!*

HARRIET. I'm not moving one step until I get an explanation!

GRACE. (*As if the situation were absolutely normal and pleasant.*) *What* is there to *explain?*

HARRIET. Well, for one thing, why is this man in his underwear?

GRACE. (*Thoughtful.*) Now, *that's* something to explain! (*Muses half a beat, then brightens and explains:*) Because he's a gentleman!

WALTER. I don't follow that.

GRACE. Well, he couldn't very well take it *all* off! Could he?

HARRIET. But why did he take *anything* off?

ALEX. Grace insisted.

WALTER. (*To* GRACE, *stunned.*) Grace!

HARRIET. Oh, Grace!

GRACE. Oh, stop it, all of you! It was all perfectly logical!

WALTER. *What* was?

GRACE. *It!*

WALTER. *What?*

HARRIET. Don't *you* know?

WALTER. Well, it was pretty dark in here.

ALEX. If you people will just listen—

GRACE. —we can clear it right up!

ALEX. It was thirty below zero outside—

GRACE. He was all wet—

ALEX. She had a loaded gun—

GRACE. I was ready for the volcano— (WALTER *brightens;* HARRIET *and* ALEX *go blank.*)

HARRIET and ALEX. What?!

GRACE. Alex, it's no use. Harriet, can't we just forget the whole thing happened?

HARRIET. Oh, how I wish I could! My little sister, cavorting around in her nightgown—

GRACE. This is not a nightgown, it's a *costume!*

HARRIET. Somebody's having a *ball?*

WALTER and ALEX. (*One backstep.*) Not *me!*

GRACE. You're jumping to conclusions!

HARRIET. I'm not jumping, I'm being pushed.

GRACE. Harriet, if you must know— (*Conspiratorially.*) This man arrived at my door soaking wet. He'd had a blow on the head and lost his memory . . . he couldn't remember his name . . . but these men were after him, and—and— (*Sees disbelief on all faces; stops.*) Oh, all right! (*Gestures dramatically at* ALEX.) *This* man is— my *husband!*

ALEX. Huh? Oh. Grace—do you *really* think you ought to *tell* her that?

GRACE. (*Sotto voce.*) Do you have a better idea?

ALEX. (*Similarly.*) No.

WALTER. Grace, what are you saying—?!

GRACE. Oh, Walter, it's no use pretending. Harriet would have found out my secret sooner or later.

HARRIET. But—Grace—if you're married—why keep it a secret?

GRACE. Rules! Company rules! Mutual of Pittsburgh doesn't allow married secretaries! Right, Walter?

WALTER. Uh.

HARRIET. Grace—just who *is* Walter?

GRACE. (*Points.*) Him. Walter Chepple, my boss, Harriet Larkin, my sister.

WALTER. Charmed.

HARRIET. Oh, of course. Grace has written me so much about you! But I don't understand—if Grace can't be married, why are *you* keeping her *secret?*

WALTER. She's too good a secretary to lose.

GRACE. And the pay is too good for me to quit, even though—uh—

ALEX. (*Sees she's forgotten, reminds her.*) "Alex."

GRACE. Thank you. Even though Alex has a wonderful job.

HARRIET. (*Relaxed and chatty, now, starts removing her coat; WALTER, seeing this and bowing to fate, removes his hat and coat.*) How nice. What does he do?

GRACE. Uh.

WALTER. (*Bewildered by her reticence.*) Go on, Grace. Tell her.

GRACE. You *know* what he does?

WALTER. (*Very much at sea.*) Of course I know. Of course—I never did see his identification card . . .

GRACE. You mean—a card that tells what *he* does for a living?!

WALTER. Naturally!

ALEX. (*Enjoying her discomfiture.*) Have to carry one at all times. It's the law. (*Remembers.*) Hey! My wallet's still in my pants! My credit cards will melt! (*Rushes to oven, retrieves shirt, jacket and pants, during:*)

HARRIET. (*Holding out coat uncertainly.*) Grace, where do I—?

GRACE. Oh, here, give me those things, both of you. (*Takes* HARRIET's *coat,* WALTER's *hat and coat.*) I'll put them in on the bed. (*Heads for curtains.*) Walter, would you . . . fix everybody a *drink* or something?!

WALTER. (*As she exits.*) Sure thing. I know *I* can use one! What does everybody want?

ALEX. (*Donning trousers and shirt.*) What have you got?

HARRIET. (*Sitting in chair Left of table.*) Don't *you* know, Mister—uh—?

ALEX. Docker. But you really must call me Alex, now that we're in-laws. May I call you Harriet?

HARRIET. Oh, certainly, Alex. But tell me—what *do* you do for a living? We got sidetracked a moment ago.

ALEX. (*After a quick glance toward bedroom.*) Telephone repairman. But I'd prefer you didn't discuss it in front of Grace. She's—a little ashamed that I'm not a big executive.

WALTER. (*Now at counter, about to fix drinks.*) Speaking of Grace, what's keeping her? How long could it take to put coats on a bed?

ALEX. Search me. How big is the bedroom?

HARRIET. Don't *you* know?

ALEX. Uh. Well, you see— (*Stops gratefully as* GRACE *comes out again.*) Oh, hi there, honey.

HARRIET. Grace, this is so exciting, you must sit down and tell me simply everything!

WALTER. (*As* GRACE *sits uneasily on other chair opposite* HARRIET.) Hold it just a minute—I'm still waiting for drink orders. Grace, I know *you* like straight whiskey on the rocks—

ALEX. She does?

HARRIET. Don't *you* know?

GRACE. There wasn't time to tell him. Everything's been so confusing—keeping the truth from the rest of the office, dashing out for a secret ceremony—!

HARRIET. But Grace—you could at least have written to Mother!

GRACE. Oh, I know I should have, but—well—

ALEX. There wasn't time!

GRACE. That's right! We just didn't have time!

HARRIET. How long could it take?

ALEX. Too long. You see—we just got married this afternoon!

WALTER. (*Sardonically "helpful."*) On her coffee break!

HARRIET. Grace! This is your *wedding night?!* How could you let me intrude?!

GRACE. I *told* you to go to a *hotel!*

HARRIET. I wish I had!

WALTER. Nonsense! We wouldn't hear of it. We'd love to have you stay here, with us.

HARRIET, GRACE, and ALEX. *"Us?"*

WALTER. A figure of speech. I meant the group of us wouldn't think of sending you to a hotel. I remember remarking at the wedding, "If Harriet shows up, let's *not* send her to a hotel!" *Didn't* I, Alex?!

ALEX. I was so nervous, I didn't hear a word you said.

HARRIET. Oh, now I see! Walter, *you* are the *best man!*

WALTER. (*With extra meaning, answers her, but glares at* ALEX.) I hope to tell you!

HARRIET. But why is he here on your wedding night?

WALTER. Why not? *You're* here on their wedding night . . . !

ALEX. (*Elaborately yawns and stretches.*) Yes, and it's getting late . . .

GRACE. (*As* HARRIET *starts to rise.*) *Wait!* (*Startled,* HARRIET *sits again.*) We didn't even have that drink yet! Walter—?

WALTER. Straight whiskey on the rocks okay all around?

ALEX. Fine by me.

GRACE. Oh, absolutely.

HARRIET. Uh, yes, thank you. (*To* GRACE, *as* WALTER *prepares drinks, which he will hand out when he is*

finished with all of them.) Now, Grace, you simply must
tell me everything! Where did you and Mister Docker
meet?

GRACE. Who's Mister Docker?

ALEX. I am.

GRACE. (*Does a take at him, then quickly turns back
to* HARRIET, *and "covers:"*) It was a whirlwind romance.
We never used last names.

ALEX. It was more romantic that way.

HARRIET. (*Not convinced, but polite.*) I see.

ALEX. Well, if you'll excuse me, I'm going to hang my
jacket in our bedroom closet.

GRACE. Wardrobe.

ALEX. Wardrobe. (*Starts for curtains.*)

GRACE. (*Suddenly remembering something, comes to
her feet on:*) No! No, don't go near the wardrobe!
(*Takes jacket from a surprise-frozen* ALEX.) Let me. It's
a wife's duty! (*Rushes out through curtains with jacket.*)

ALEX. (*To* HARRIET, *smiling to cover his confusion.*)
You'd think she had a *man* in there!

WALTER. It wouldn't surprise *me!* Here— (*Comes to*
ALEX *with two drinks, hands him one,. returns to hand
other to* HARRIET, *during:*)

HARRIET. I hope it's not too late to get a room at a
hotel. . . .

WALTER. Oh, I'm sure they'd love to have you stay on
the sofa. Please say you will. I insist.

ALEX and HARRIET. *You* insist?!

GRACE. (*Pops back through curtains, anxiously.*) I hope
nobody did any talking while I was gone?

ALEX. (*Puts a friendly arm across her shoulders.*) Only
about where Harriet is going to spend the night.

GRACE. (*Reacts to arm, starts thinking ahead, says
frantically:*) *Here!* She's staying *here!* Where *else* would
my very own sister stay but *here?*

ALEX. She can't use *our* bed, darling. We barely have
room for the overcoats! (*Abruptly goes to her coat, scarf*

and beret on Right chair.) Oh, here, you forgot your *own* things. Is there room in the wardrobe?

GRACE. (*Tensely smiling, tug-of-wars with him over garments.*) No, I'll just put these on the bed!

ALEX. No, let me do it. It's a husband's duty. (*Gets garments away from her, starts for curtains.*) Describe the bed so I can find it.

GRACE. (*Starts desperately after him.*) You'll never find it alone! I'm coming with you! (*Is stopped by* WALTER'S *hand on her arm as* ALEX *exits.*)

WALTER. (*Too softly for* ALEX *to hear, but loud enough for* HARRIET.) Grace, before I lose my mind— What in the world are you hiding from Alex in that wardrobe?!

GRACE. My television set! (*Tugs free, dashes for curtains.*) Do you want him to think I'm *D—U—M?!* (*Exits, returns instantly for:*) *—B?!* (*Exits.*)

HARRIET. (*As* WALTER *turns back toward her.*) Walter —now's our chance!

WALTER. (*Takes a backstep as she stands up.*) Good grief, lady, I hardly *know* you!

HARRIET. (*Indignant at his inference.*) Our chance to get *out* of here and leave the newlyweds *alone!*

WALTER. In the *bedroom?!*

HARRIET. Where else?

WALTER. And just what do we do for hats and coats?

HARRIET. Oh, dear, you're right. But wait—! Do you have a car? Does it have a heater?

WALTER. You're proposing we make a mad dash for it? No way. I came in here with a hat and coat, and that's the way I'm leaving!

HARRIET. How can you butt in where you're not wanted?!

WALTER. (*Shrugs.*) I'm in the insurance business!

HARRIET. (*About to reply, spots pistol on table, picks it up.*) What's *this—!?*

WALTER. (*Sardonically quiet.*) It was a shotgun wedding. (*When her expression disputes this, shrugs again.*)

All right, so it was a dumb joke—but that was a pretty dumb question, too! What do you mean, "What's *this!?*" It's a pistol, of course!

HARRIET. Oh, button your lip, Chepple! (*Puts pistol back on table.*) You know darned well I mean what's it doing *here!* . . . And why did she have to use it to get her husband out of his pants? . . . And how come he mustn't know she has a TV hidden in the wardrobe? . . .

WALTER. (*Interrupts her tirade by gripping her arm, shooting a quick look toward the bedroom, then lowering his voice for:*) Listen, Harriet, I'd like some of those answers myself! But first—I've got to talk to Grace. Alone.

HARRIET. On her wedding night? If we had any decency at all, we'd get *out* of here!

WALTER. (*Urgently, keeping his voice down.*) No-no, that's exactly what we *mustn't* do! We can't leave Grace here alone with Alex!

HARRIET. (*Brightens, beams, points finger.*) *Wal*ter *Chep*ple! . . . You're *jealous!*

WALTER. (*All the more insulted because it's true.*) Over another man's bride? Don't be ridiculous!

HARRIET. (*Laughs at her own shortsightedness.*) I should've spotted it the moment I walked in! The way you *look* at her—the way you *bristle* each time he *touches* her—!

WALTER. (*Her voice is rising, and he desperately holds his forefinger to her lips for silence, as he pleads in a hoarse whisper.*) You don't understand! *Grace* doesn't want to be alone with him, *either!*

HARRIET. (*This gets to her.*) Wh-what? The man she just married—?! Of *course* she wants to be alone with him! What are you saying?

WALTER. I know it sounds crazy. I don't understand it myself. He must have some sort of *hold* over her—or *she's* got a hold on *him*—!

HARRIET. Well, it *is* their wedding night—!

WALTER. Not *that* kind of hold! Harriet—don't take *my* word for it—take your cue from *Grace:* Just *try* to go to a hotel, and *see* what she does! Oops, here they come! (*Breaks away from her, stands smiling innocently as* ALEX *and* GRACE *re-enter through curtains.*) Uh. Hi, there, lovebirds!

GRACE. Sorry to keep you waiting. It was hard finding a coat hanger in the dark.

HARRIET. Why didn't you put the light on?

GRACE. Uh. I didn't want him to see my bedroom. It's a mess.

HARRIET. *Your* bedroom—?

ALEX. She means *our* bedroom, of course. Newlywed.

WALTER. Nervous bride.

ALEX. (*Smiles ingratiatingly at* HARRIET.) *You* know what *wedding* nights are like!

HARRIET. (*Flutters.*) Not *yet*, I don't.

WALTER. Maybe you should stick around.

GRACE. (*With false-sounding tinkle of laughter.*) *Ah*-ha-ha! Oh, Walter! *Ah*-ha-ha!

HARRIET. (*With a snappish glare at* WALTER, *assures* GRACE:) Don't worry, dear, I'm clearing out right now.

GRACE. (*With instant panic.*) *No!* (*And just as instantly a charming hostess as* HARRIET *reacts.*) I mean—so *soon?* You've only just arrived!

HARRIET. (*After a quick, but now more uneasy than angry, glance toward* WALTER, *whose face is saying "I told you so!"*) Grace—are you really sure about—that is—*do* you want me to stay, or what?

GRACE. (*Her manner confirming* WALTER'S *diagnosis to* HARRIET.) Uh—well—after all—you *did* come all the from Chillicothe, and you must be *terribly* tired after such a long, long trip—?!

ALEX. Darling, it's not as though she *walked!*

GRACE. But—her first night in town . . . ? And it's so late to call a cab!

ALEX. Don't worry, dearest. I'm sure *Walter* won't

mind giving her a lift, *will* you, Walt, old man!? (*There is just the tiniest extra stress on "old man" and* WALTER *gets the not-quite-subliminal message and bridles.*)

HARRIET. (*By now quite convinced something's up.*) Nonsense, I wouldn't *hear* of putting him to all that trouble. I'll stay! (*Picks up her suitcase and heads for curtains.*) I'll just put this into the bedroom!

ALEX. (*A bit surprised by her sudden change of mood.*) *Our* bedroom—?

HARRIET. (*Pauses at curtain for:*) How many you got?! (*Exits with suitcase;* ALEX *and* WALTER *immediately converge upon* GRACE, *both speaking rapidly in lowered voices.*)

WALTER. Grace, what *is* it with you and this guy?! *Wedding* night! Good grief!

GRACE. I *had* to say *something* when Harriet saw us *dressed* like that!

ALEX. I think you behaved splendidly, Grace. And thinking it up so *fast!* I *knew* you had a brilliant mind the moment we met! (GRACE, *of course, absolutely melts, staring adoringly at him, but blinks the mood away as* WALTER *starts in on* ALEX:)

WALTER. Listen, I don't know what your angle is, but if you think I'll leave this helpless girl alone with you, you're crazy!

ALEX. Well, you're *just* as crazy if you think I'll leave her alone with *you!*

WALTER. (*At* last *he knows why* ALEX *is still hanging around.*) So *that's* it!

GRACE. *What's* it? (*But both men ignore her, now that they have openly declared war.*)

ALEX. Any *man* who'd have a lovely young girl *dressed* like that—!

WALTER. Any man who'd get *undressed* in *front* of a lovely young girl like that!

ALEX. I was all wet!

WALTER. You still are!

GRACE. Boys, boys! Harriet will hear you!

ALEX. (*Incredulously.*) *Who* you calling a *boy—?!*

ALEX and WALTER. (*Without pause completing* ALEX's *line, pointing at other man.*) *—him?*

GRACE. Oh, for heaven's sake—!

WALTER. Grace, you are *not* staying here *alone* with this man!

ALEX. How can I leave on our wedding night? Won't Harriet think it's strange?

GRACE. Yes. Walter, she *will.*

WALTER. I've got it! Grace, you and Alex can have a tiff, and Alex can walk out!

ALEX. Grace, a man *never* walks out on his *wedding* night!

WALTER. So set a precedent!

ALEX. But what could we possibly *tiff* about? (*Then they all have their answer in the person of* HARRIET, *as she re-enters; all three react, trying to look normal and casual.*)

HARRIET. (*Has stopped just inside room, points back toward curtains.*) Grace—there's a *kitchen sink* in your bathroom—!

WALTER. Alex, I wouldn't *stand* for that kind of criticism from a guest! If I were *you,* I'd *leave!*

GRACE. But there *is* a kitchen sink in my bathroom—?! And—after all, she's *family* . . .

WALTER. See, Alex? It's always the same old story— you think you're marrying a *person,* but you're really marrying a whole *family!* If I were *you,* I'd *walk out!*

ALEX. But I *like* my new family. Don't *you?*

WALTER. Uh. Well, sure. Of course I do. I like Harriet very much!

HARRIET. Why, thank you, Walter!

ALEX. Why don't you *show* her how much, by driving her to a hotel?

HARRIET. Oh, that won't be necessary.

WALTER. I don't mind at all. Of course, I'd like *Alex* to come along to keep me *company* on the ride *back*.

HARRIET. (*To* WALTER.) *You're* coming back *here* tonight?

WALTER. Well, I have to bring the lucky man back to his bride!

GRACE. Oh, that's all right, Walter, you don't have to.

HARRIET. You don't want Alex back?

GRACE. It'll be pretty late by then. I'll probably be in bed.

HARRIET. (*In poignant confusion.*) *Alone?*

GRACE. (*With sincere longing.*) I certainly hope so! (*PHONE rings; a disgruntled* WALTER *starts toward it; to* WALTER:) If it's Estelle, make sure you tell her you've got your shoes on!

HARRIET. (*As* WALTER *stops for one second to give a baffled look back at* GRACE.) Who is Estelle?

GRACE. You wouldn't like her. (*PHONE rings again;* WALTER *starts for it again.*)

HARRIET. But why would Walter be here without his shoes on?

ALEX. *Grace* is here without shoes on . . . !

GRACE. (*As* WALTER *picks up phone, looks down at her feet.*) I *thought* it was kind of chilly in here! I'll be back in a minute! (*Hurries off through curtains, during:*)

WALTER. (*On phone.*) Hello? . . . Who? . . . Why— yes—he's still here. Just a moment. (*Extends phone toward* ALEX, *who is already moving that way.*) Somebody named Marge at the phone company . . .

ALEX. Oh. Thanks. (*Takes phone, speaks into it.*) Hi, Marge. . . . *What?* Aw, come *on!* I was ready for a shower and a hot bed—! (WALTER—*headed back to* HAR-RIET—*reacts, and so does she, at* ALEX's *inadvertent tongue-twist, which he hastily corrects:*) I mean a hot shower and bed! . . . But that's halfway across Queens! . . . Oh, sure, sure. I will. It's just that—it's kind of an awkward time to— (*Glances toward others, decides not to finish; listens; then:*) Yeah, yeah, I got the address. . . . Will do. Thanks. (*Hangs up, turns to face the others, smiling but abashed.*) Uh. Emergency. Have to get over there right now . . .

HARRIET. *Tonight?* What's the telephone company *thinking* of?!

ALEX. Uh—well, you see—they don't know it's my *wedding* night.

WALTER. (*Pleased at the development, gallantly helps* ALEX *along, with:*) Don't forget, Harriet, the wedding was a *secret!*

HARRIET. I thought that was just from the *insurance* company. Doesn't the *phone company* approve of marriage, *either?*

WALTER. Bad for business. Newlyweds usually leave the phone off the hook.

(*All look toward curtains as* GRACE *re-enters; she has doffed the anklets, lei, and flower in her hair, and the grass skirt, too, but we cannot see this because she's in a robe and a pair of flat-soled fuzzy slippers.*)

GRACE. Boy, it sure feels good to get that grass skirt off! (*Looks puzzledly at* ALEX *as he starts for curtains.*)

ALEX. Excuse me, I have to get my jacket.

GRACE. (*Bars his way, instantly.*) *No!* I mean, *I'll* get it!

ALEX. (*Baffled but agreeable.*) Uh—why, sure. Whatever you say.

GRACE. Be right back! (*Vanishes through curtains.*)

ALEX. (*Turns to face others, smiles awkwardly.*) Helpful, isn't she!

HARRIET. Sending you out on a night like this! (*As* GRACE *pops back into room with jacket.*) I think it's criminal! (GRACE *reacts.*)

ALEX. Well, when there's a *job* to do— (*Senses* GRACE, *turns, reaches for jacket.*) Oh. Thanks.

GRACE. (*Had been holding jacket out at arm's length, but now pulls it sharply back against her breast, eyes wide with suspicion.*) "A *job* to do?" Who? *You? To-night?!* You're pulling another job?!

WALTER. (*Pleased* ALEX *is departing.*) Grace, the man has to earn his living. . . . "*Pulling*" a job—?!

ALEX. (*With panicky haste.*) That's the latest slang! Like at a *switchboard*—push-*pull*-push-*pull*—?! Work-work-work!

GRACE. (*Thrusts jacket out at* ALEX.) Here you go, darling! Work hard. Hurry home. I'll be waiting.

ALEX. (*Who has turned his back to her and allowed her to assist him into jacket, now looks hopefully back at her, on:*) You will?

HARRIET. (*Bewildered.*) Of *course* she will. Where *else* would she be?

GRACE. I mean waiting *up*—that is—if he doesn't take *too* long . . .

ALEX. Believe me, I won't! (*Will gather up boots and tools, during:*) I'll move so fast, they won't even know I've *been* there!

GRACE. (*Grabs up pistol like helpful wife, hands it to him, on:*) Oh, I hope so! (*He hastily pockets it before others can see it.*) Then when you come back—I want to have a long talk with you!

WALTER. What's there to *talk* about?!

ALEX. (*Moving toward front door.*) My occupation. She's always after me to get into another line of work.

HARRIET. Why, what's *wrong* with what you do?

GRACE. Harriet! Do you mean—you *know* what he does for a living? How did you find out?!

WALTER. (*At sea.*) Alex *told* her, of course. Shortly after she got here.

GRACE. (*To* HARRIET.) And—you don't *mind*—?!

HARRIET. (*It seems the sensible thing to say.*) Why

should I? *Every* man can't be a *business* executive . . .
(*As* GRACE *gapes in bewilderment, the PHONE rings.*)

ALEX. (*Near door.*) If that's Marge, again, tell her I'm
on my way—!

GRACE. (*This is the first time she's heard the name,
and she reacts as any woman would who learns that
there's a woman she didn't know about in the life of a
man she likes.*) "Marge—?"

ALEX. (*Catches her tone, becomes instantly matter-of-
fact.*) You don't know her, honey. She—uh—she's a
business associate at the— (*Stops, realizing* GRACE *must
not talk with* MARGE; *PHONE rings again, he dashes
back across room.*) Here, *I'd* better talk to her—

GRACE. (*Almost gallops for phone, beats him to it.*)
No-no! I'll get it! I'd like very much to talk to this—
Marge! (*Realizes how jealous this sounds, stops with her
hand on phone, but without picking it up, to say airily
to* HARRIET:) A wife should take an *interest* in her husband's *work.* . . . (*PHONE rings again, she yanks it up
to her ear, but* WALTER *speaks before she does.*)

WALTER. (*Incredulous.*) *Interest?* Looks more like an
obsession!

GRACE. (*Grimaces at his remark, but speaks in normal
voice on phone:*) Hello? . . . Oh! Yes, he's here! . . .
Just a moment, please—! (*Her face has brightened im-
measurably, as she calls across room:*) It's for you,
Walter.

WALTER. (*Very surprised, starts toward her.*) Me?
Who in the world knows I'm *here*—? (*As he and* GRACE
*maneuver to change positions—since it is very close
quarters over by the phone—*ALEX *takes this opportunity
to step quickly to* HARRIET, *unnoticed by the others, and
speaks quickly in a low, urgent voice.*)

ALEX. Listen, I don't have time to explain, now, but—
whatever you do—*don't* leave here! Grace must *not* be
left alone with Walter! Can't explain now. Trust me.

(*While* HARRIET *is trying to get a look of comprehension over her look of utter confusion,* WALTER *finally gets on the phone, and* GRACE *starts back toward others, who draw slightly apart.*)

WALTER. Hello? . . . Oh, *hi,* Lydia! Gosh, I'm awful sorry about not being there, with the party and everything, but . . . *What?!* All the way from Pittsburgh? . . . He *isn't!* . . . Oh, damn! (*Covers mouthpiece, his face pale with panic, tells others:*) She says the chairman of the board is coming by to shake my hand! . . . What am I going to *do?!*

ALEX. Bring your camera. If he gets smashed out of his skull, you can sell him the film at a handsome profit. (WALTER *gives him a scathing narrow-eyed glance, but gets back on the phone as* GRACE *starts toward curtains.*)

GRACE. I'll get your things—

WALTER. (*On phone again, as she exits.*) Of *course* I'll be there, Lydia! Intended to come all along, just got slightly delayed. . . . Figure about—oh . . . fifteen minutes . . . Right! See you! (*Hangs up, smiles lamely at* HARRIET *and* ALEX.) Gotta go. Party.

ALEX. (*As if prefixed by* "That's a—") Shame. We'll miss you. (*Shakes his head as if sorry, a patent falsification at which* WALTER *quietly glowers, as* GRACE *re-enters with his overcoat and homburg; he starts out of phone area, takes them, dons them, during:*)

GRACE. But Walter—who told Lydia where to find you?

WALTER. I think it must've been Estelle.

GRACE. Why?

WALTER. Lydia said, "Chepple, put your shoes on and get over here!"

HARRIET. Walter, why does this Estelle seem to think you're running around with no shoes on?

GRACE. Because that's what *I* told her.

WALTER. For pete's sake, *why?!*

GRACE. It was an honest mistake . . .

WALTER. (*Wearily waves her to silence before she can continue, picks up his camera from sofa and starts for door, during:*) I'm sure it was. It always is. Like the time she typed up an important letter to the zone vice president, over my signature, telling him the city fathers wanted him to be grand marshal in the Veteran's Day parade!

GRACE. Oh. That.

ALEX. What happened?

WALTER. (*Stops in doorway, and says:*) She didn't *say* "Veteran's Day." To save time, *she* just used the *initials!* (*As others react, and* GRACE *gives a smile-and-shrug of acute embarrassment,* WALTER *rolls his eyes heavenward and exits.*)

ALEX. (*Speaking to* GRACE.) I gotta get going. Keep this door locked till I get back, hear? (*Almost steps out door, but* GRACE *runs to him, grabs his hand.*)

GRACE. Alex—! *Must* you? Can't we have that talk *now?*

ALEX. Just this one last job, tonight, and then I'll talk until the sun comes up, if you like.

GRACE. Well . . . all right . . . but *please* be careful! I don't know what I'd do if you got caught—!

HARRIET. "Caught—?"

ALEX. Sometimes my pants get snagged when I climb through a window.

HARRIET. Oh . . . ?

ALEX. (*To* GRACE.) Now, don't worry about a thing. This shouldn't take me long, maybe an hour or two. (*Pulling his hand away, back-stepping toward doorway.*) And don't you worry your pretty little head about a thing while I'm gone, understand?

GRACE. (*Though reluctant, takes a back-step herself, says quietly:*) . . . Okay. (*They look at each other for a moment, while* HARRIET *stands watching them impassively, and then—and it is all at once the most natural thing in the world—they each step forward at the same moment, and go into a brief-but-thorough embrace, stare into one another's eyes a moment, and then* ALEX *releases her and hurries off through the doorway without another word;* GRACE *just stands where she is, immobile, then senses* HARRIET *is watching, blinks herself back to reality, and with a shy little laugh, shuts the door matter-of-factly, and sighs.*) He's terribly romantic.

HARRIET. He leaves you alone on your wedding night and he's *romantic—?!*

GRACE. (*Starts to bustle about, picking up anything that needs picking up—used drink-glasses, etc.—which she will shortly take off through curtains with her.*) There's a lot more to love than just bedding down together. When a man and a woman feel a certain way about each other—*anything* the other one *does* is romantic. I wouldn't swap the look he gave me, just before he walked through that door, for two weeks on the Riviera with Robert Redford! (*Exits, then returns.*) Well . . . *one* week! (*Re-exits.*)

HARRIET. (*Absorbs this, standing where she is; and then—abruptly and unexpectedly—her manner changes; she is suddenly in what is obviously a nail-biting and lip-nibbling mood, and her manner is decidedly furtive as she gives one more glance at the still-swaying bead curtains, then scurries to the phone, grabs it up, dials furiously, and keeps an eye and ear cocked toward* GRACE'S *possible return, while she—as soon as her party gets on the line—speaks in a low and urgent voice:*) Hello? . . . Gregor! My darling! . . . What do you mean, "Who is this?"!—it's Harriet! . . . Yes, I'm at Grace's apartment! . . . No, she doesn't know a thing about it. . . . Yes, hurry, darling, hurry! . . . And wait till you see what I brought us as a wedding present! It's from Mother! . . . She doesn't *know* it, yet, but she always promised it to me if I ever got married, and— What? . . . Yes, you're right, I *am* wasting time! I didn't think! By all means, get over here! . . . Yes, Gregor, I adore you, too! . . . Now hurry! (*Hangs up, sighs, then recovers her composure and much of her earlier impassive attitude, and has crossed back to the table by the time* GRACE *re-enters, empty-handed, through curtains.*) Grace . . . there's something I'd like to bring up—!

GRACE. (*Looks Upstage.*) Well, there's something I'd like to take down! (*Turns back to face* HARRIET, *hopefully.*) I'm getting awfully tired of tripping over the table . . . (*Hastens off through curtains.*)

HARRIET. You're going to take down the *table*—?!

GRACE. (*Off.*) No. The Christmas tree!

HARRIET. (*Looks up in surprise as* GRACE *re-enters with* HARRIET'S *suitcase.*) Grace, what are you doing with that?

GRACE. Since you decided to stay the night, I thought I'd bring this back to you. (*Raises it with an effort and sets it onto table.*) It's too dark to change in the bedroom.

HARRIET. Why don't you put the light on?

GRACE. I can't find it. The bulb, I mean. I unscrewed it so Alex wouldn't accidentally turn on the light and see the TV set in the wardrobe. Now I can't locate it. It must have rolled, or something. (*Heads back for curtains.*) I hope I can recognize the ornament-box by feel. (*Exits.*)

HARRIET. Grace, that's another thing—why can't your husband know you have a TV?

GRACE. (*Off.*) Because he might want to *watch* it, and this is our *wedding* night!

HARRIET. Oh.

GRACE. (*Off. Half to herself.*) Now where in the world did that box disappear to—?! (*We hear a loud Offstage POP; as* HARRIET *reacts:*) Well—I found the light bulb!

HARRIET. (*As* GRACE *emerges through curtains, lifts one slippered foot and starts checking the sole for damage.*) Are you all right—?

GRACE. That's what I'm trying to find out . . . !

(*Satisfied, returns foot to the floor, starts for cabinet beneath hutch.*) But I'd better clean up the mess before I forget and walk through it barefoot— (*Will remove whisk broom, dustpan and flashlight from cabinet.*) Let's see now—if I hold the pan in this hand, sweep with that hand, and the end of the flashlight in my mouth—!

HARRIET. Why don't you just ask *me* to help?

GRACE. Habit, I guess. I've been living *alone* too long. . . . *Much* too long. (*Starts for bedroom.*) Well, c'mon, let's get it over with—

HARRIET. (*Stops her with hand on arm, reminded by* GRACE's *first remark.*) Wait—Grace, you know what you said about living alone too long—?

GRACE. Oh, Harriet, I don't want to talk about Alex right now—!

HARRIET. It's not about Alex. It's about me. (*Takes her hand from* GRACE's *arm, and turns away, facing toward Downstage Left, but* GRACE *remains in place, too intrigued by* HARRIET's *attitude to continue off to bedroom.*) I've been living alone much too long, myself. I— I came to New York to *do* something about it . . . !

GRACE. (*Not an invitation, but a declaration of suspected fact.*) You're moving in with *me*. . . .

HARRIET. (*Reacts, turns to face her once again.*) Well, hardly! What would your *husband* think?

GRACE. Oh. Oh, yeah. That's right . . . Well, look, I'm sure that if I talked it over with Alex—

HARRIET. But, darling, that's what I've been trying to tell you! I'm going to *have* a place to stay. A place of my own. As soon as *Gregor* gets here . . . !

GRACE. *Who?*

HARRIET. Gregor Vanitzky, the man I'm going to marry!

GRACE. (*Abruptly depositing pan, brush and flashlight on sofa, and going to* HARRIET *with outstretched hands and taking hers.*) Oh, darling, congratulations! I'm so happy for you! But tell me—where did you meet him—?

HARRIET. (*Rapturously.*) In his *tent.*

GRACE. His *tent?*

HARRIET. Where he holds revival meetings. He's an evangelist! In Hammerson's corn field.

GRACE. Tell me all about it, Harriet! I'm so excited! Imagine *you* getting *married*—of all *people*—at *your* age—!

HARRIET. (*Rather icily withdraws her hands from* GRACE'S *grip.*) It's not exactly a *miracle*, Grace . . . !

GRACE. But *I* didn't mean—

HARRIET. (*Too ecstatic to stay mad.*) Oh, I know, darling, I know! (*Softens even more, her face aglow at the memory, rhapsodizing.*) Oh, but it was marvelous! I was in the front row—watching his incredible face—listening to his ringing words—hypnotized by his eloquent hands—then, all at once, he said— (*A solemn imitation of his tone.*) "Who among *you* can declare freedom from the corruption of *sin?!*" (*Sighs, then gives a little shrug.*) So I stood up.

GRACE. You *what?!*

HARRIET. I didn't know it was a rhetorical question. And I did so want to make a good impression—!

GRACE. What happened?

HARRIET. Well, he stopped talking, of course. Then somebody laughed—then somebody else—and all at once, everybody in the place was laughing—! I absolutely could have *died* of embarrassment, Grace!

GRACE. Oh, you poor darling! What did you do?

HARRIET. I very nearly turned and ran—but then—I noticed something—something that made all the difference: *Gregor* wasn't laughing. He stared at me—then he held out his hands toward me—and all at once, all the laughter subsided—and then there was this glorious silence—and then and there—in the middle of all the quiet —he said, "Yes! Yes, I can feel the truth of it! I can see the glory of your soul shining through your eyes!"

GRACE. Oh, Harriet, how marvelous!

HARRIET. Then he had me come up to the platform and

stand beside him, and I stayed there for the whole meet-
ing, and everybody prayed and sang and cheered for hours
and hours—and then, when it was all over—and all the
crowds had gone home—Gregor took my hands, looked
into my eyes, and said, "How would you like to split a
pizza?!"

GRACE. Oh, Harriet! That's the most romantic thing
I ever heard!

HARRIET. (*Snaps out of her ecstasy, shrugs away the
rest.*) So we did, and we talked and talked, and one thing
led to another, and then when he said he was bringing
his movement to New York, I knew I had to follow him,
so— Here I am! And he's coming here tonight, to claim
me as his bride! I can't wait for him to meet you and
Alex—!

GRACE. (*The horror of the situation strikes her.*)
Alex?! . . . Oh—but—Gregor *mustn't* meet *Alex—!*

HARRIET. For heaven's sake, darling, why not?

GRACE. Harriet, what are you *thinking* of? You *know*
what Alex does for a *living!* How can you tell *Gregor?!*

HARRIET. Grace, I'm surprised at you! A wife should
never be ashamed of what her husband does for a living
—after all, in the last analysis, he's doing it for you!
That's all that matters.

GRACE. It *is?*

HARRIET. (*Takes her hand, pats it fondly.*) Of course
it is!

GRACE. (*Laughs, baffled but pleased.*) Honestly, Harriet, you're too much! Now, look, darling, you just relax,
while I clean up that mess, and find the box for those
ornaments! (GRACE *exits through curtains.*)

HARRIET. (*Is about to reply, when there comes a soft
KNOCK at the door; she reacts with a gasp of joyous
anticipation, then smooths her dress a second and pats
at her hair, then starts for door, but a moment before
touching the knob, she remembers something, withdraws
her hand, and instead says softly, very close to the door,*

looking anxiously back toward curtains:) Just a minute,
my darling! (*She rushes to suitcase on table, opens it,
and removes a gleaming four-piece silver service: tray,
coffee urn, sugar bowl and creamer; it takes but a moment to set the suitcase on the chair, Left; the KNOCK
sounds again, a little louder; she hastily sets the three
serving-pieces onto the tray, then hurries to the door,
speaking as she does so:*) Come to me, my beloved—!
(*Her arms, outflung in amorous greeting, remain that
way not more than an instant, and she gapes in bewilderment as* ALEX *steps in the door, smiling but wary of her
momentary attitude.*) Alex!

ALEX. (*A little cautiously, not yet closing the door behind him.*) Hi, there—Harriet— That was—uh—some
greeting you just gave me . . . !

HARRIET. Our family—is very friendly. (*Smiles awkwardly;* ALEX, *sensing he's safe from her, shuts door.*)
But—what are you doing *here*?

ALEX. (*Shucking out of his jacket, which he will set
on back of chair, Left, semi-shrouding the suitcase.*)
The stupid *truck* wouldn't start! I think it's gas-line
freeze. But whatever it is, I'd better tell Marge, so she
can dispatch someone else in my place! (*Heads for phone,
asking almost incuriously:*) Where's Grace?

HARRIET. Getting out the ornament box. We were going
to take down the tree.

ALEX. (*Will get to phone and start dialing.*) *Walter*
hasn't come nosing around again, has he—?

HARRIET. Didn't he say he was going to a party—?

ALEX. Yeah, he *said* that . . . but he might suddenly
change his mind, and— (*Interrupts himself as his call is
received, speaks on phone:*) Marge? Alex. . . . Engine
trouble. You'd better send somebody else . . . (*As he is
speaking, there comes a soft KNOCK at the door which
he does not hear, but* HARRIET *does, and she reacts; taking only a second to assure herself that his back is to the
door, she hastily opens it, and* GREGOR VANITZKY *steps*

*in, his arms flung wide to embrace her; we have just
enough time to see that* GREGOR *is tall, his face somewhat
theatrically sinister of aspect despite his smile of rapture,
and his graying hair flaring back in a more-than-medium-
length rumpled-fur fashion that—were he wearing a cloak
—would pinpoint him as a mad scientist, at least, or a
prowling vampire, at best; but he is dressed—as we'll
later see—in meticulous and expensive clothing under-
neath his tailored topcoat, which is all we can see at the
moment; and it is a brief moment, too, because he is
barely across the threshold when* HARRIET—*her head and
gaze turned anxiously back toward* ALEX *on the telephone—places a palm flat upon his chest and presses him
back swiftly into the hall, herself exiting with him, and
shutting the door after them with her free hand; all this
has taken place in barely three seconds, so that the phone
conversation continues almost without pause:*) Mean-
time, if you can swing it, you might send a repair truck
out this way for a look at that engine . . . (GRACE *enters
through curtains at this moment, carrying an empty cor-
rugated-cardboard carton, and reacts to his voice, on:*)
Yeah, that's what I said—*dead, completely* dead! . . .
(*It only takes her a half-second, however, to also react
to his words, and her face is a study in stunned horror.*)
Hell, it wasn't *my* fault, Marge. How did *I* know it would
happen?! . . . (GRACE, *her face desperate with unhap-
piness, glances over and sees the silver service, reacts,
looks from him to the service, and we know she thinks
this is her "burglar's" latest haul; she moves to it,
zombie-like, unable to believe her eyes.*) Aw, c'mon,
Marge, be a pal! What's one more little *dispatchment*
between friends?! . . . Hey, thanks, you're a peach!
. . . Right! 'Bye, now! (*Hangs up, sighs with relief,
turns and sees* GRACE, *who has been watching him, her
face now almost expressionless.*) Oh, there you are,
honey—! (*Takes a pace toward her, but stops as she
drops box to floor and declares:*)

GRACE. Oh, Alex! How could you?! Burglary is bad enough, but *murder!*

ALEX. *Murder?!* What the heck are you—? (*Before he can add "—talking about?":*)

GRACE. Stop right there! Don't come near me! I heard everything. It's no use your trying to deny it!

ALEX. (*Another step her way, despite himself.*) Heard *what?* I have nothing *to* deny!

GRACE. (*Drawing herself up bravely.*) Oh, no? Then exactly what do you call *this—?! (Gestures dramatically at silver service.*) Do you deny this is what you were steal_ ing when you murdered that poor man?!

ALEX. *What* man? Grace, for pete's sake, I did not murder *anybody!* Not tonight, not ever!

GRACE. Then where did this silver service come from?!

ALEX. Search *me!*

GRACE. I'll leave *that* job to the *police!* (*This has been proud and imperious, but she turns weepy, for:*) Oh, Alex—I feel so—betrayed! I should never have let you pull that one last job! I had a premonition something terrible would happen! (*Covers her face.*)

ALEX. (*Goes to her, will gently remove her hands from her face.*) But Grace—honey—nothing terrible *did* happen! There's been no murder— And I never saw that silver before in my life!

GRACE. (*Pulls her hands from his, turns her back to him.*) Lies! Lies! Always more lies! I wanted to help you—I think I really *could* have helped you—but if you won't even be *honest* with me—?! (*Stops as he grips her shoulders and starts turning her to face him.*) Alex— what are you doing—?!

ALEX. (*Now holding her facing him.*) I'm getting ready to kiss you. (*She stares at him, and then, quickly and gently, he kisses her.*)

GRACE. (*Wide-eyed and much subdued, now.*) Why did you do that?

ALEX. Why do you think? (*Kisses her again, this time doing a slightly better job.*)

GRACE. (*Blinking and catching her breath as they break.*) Why did you do that again?

ALEX. I thought maybe *action* might tell you more about me than words! Now, I ask you—was that the kiss of a thief and murderer—?

GRACE. I'm not sure . . . (*Beat.*) Let's try it again! (*And this time, her arms go up and around his neck, and he has to hold her half for cooperation, and half for balance, as they make a thoroughly delightful job of kissing; when it is over, GRACE rests her head against his chest, her eyes closed in dreamy contentment—and ALEX is not likely to disengage his embrace, either; then suddenly her eyes open wide, and she pulls busily out of his arms, and grabs up the fallen box from the floor.*) What are we thinking of?! Time is running out, fast! (*Has begun packing silver service into box.*) We've got to hide the evidence, quickly, before the police arrive!

ALEX. What makes you think the *police* are arriving?

GRACE. What makes you think they're *not?!* (*Has silver in box, now, picks up box, looks Left and Right in desperation and confusion, then takes box off through curtains, almost in a run, on:*) You have an awful lot to learn about being a successful crook!

ALEX. (*Takes a step after her.*) But Grace—! (*Gives it up, starts for door.*) Listen, I've got to go down and wait for a repair truck, but as soon as I get back, you and I are going to have a long talk—!

GRACE. (*Off.*) *What* did you say—? (*Will emerge empty-handed through curtains, on:*) It's hard to hear you, back in the bedroom—

ALEX. (*Facing her, but starting to open door.*) Never mind. I'll tell you when I get back.

GRACE. (*Hurries toward him.*) Oh, Alex! You're not going out *again*—?! With the body barely cold?! (*Before he can reply, door has come fully open, and through it,*

GRACE—*along with us*—*sees* HARRIET *bent backward, head doorward, in* GREGOR'S *arms, in the midst of a madly passionate kiss;* GRACE *reacts.*) Harriet! What are you *doing?!*

ALEX. (*Turns and catches tableau a moment, and turns head to* GRACE *for:*) Can't you tell?

HARRIET. (*Face upside-down as she and* GREGOR *maintain backbend-embrace.*) Oh! Alex . . . Grace . . . I I'd like you to meet—my *fiance!*

ALEX. (*To* GRACE.) I must say—you Larkin girls don't waste much time—! (*They break clinch.*)

GREGOR. (*Entering room arm in arm with* HARRIET.) I beg your pardon—?

GRACE. (*Closing door.*) Alex, Harriet didn't *just* meet him! Why she's known him for—for—?

HARRIET. *Almost* an entire *week!*

ALEX. (*As if she'd said a much longer, more respectable duration, spreads his hands and gives a large, slow shrug, as if the only-slightly-longer-than-chance-meeting time makes a big difference in his initial attitude that she was a fast worker.*) Oh, *well* then!

GREGOR. (*Sensing the slight mockery.*) Sir, when one finds true love, time has no meaning.

ALEX. Is that why brides always arrive late?

GRACE. Alex!

ALEX. (*A little ashamed of himself.*) Okay, okay. (*Extends hand to* GREGOR.) Congratulations. You've got yourself a nice little lady, there, whoever you are . . . ?

GREGOR. (*As they break handshake, he gives a Prussian head-bow and heel-click, on:*) I'm sorry, my name is Gregor Vanitzky.

ALEX. (*Truly misunderstanding his meaning.*) *I'd* be sorry, *too*, why don't you *change* it?

HARRIET. *What—?!*

ALEX. (*Catching his gaffe.*) Oh! You meant—sorry you hadn't told me your name—oh boy—hey, *I'm* sorry! Things have been—a little confusing, tonight . . .

HARRIET. (*Suddenly contrite.*) Oh, my goodness, of course they have! I completely forgot—! (*To* GREGOR.) This is their wedding night!

GREGOR. (*Now embarrassed to have intruded.*) I had no idea! *I'm* sorry—! . . . Mister—? (*Doesn't know the name to tag onto the apology.*)

ALEX. (*Realizing his lapse.*) *I'm* sorry! Docker. Alex Docker.

HARRIET. (*Realizes her sister has not been introduced.*) Oh, and *I'm* sorry, this is my sister Grace!

GRACE. (*Taking his hand briefly.*) Isn't this the *sorriest* bunch of people! (*This sets them all laughing, and they start down toward sofa area, their mutual mood more convivial.*) Listen, Alex darling, why don't you fix us all a drink—?

HARRIET. Grace! *Gregor* doesn't drink!

GRACE. Oh, of course! *I'm* sorry—!

GREGOR. Let's not start *that* again!

ALEX. Are you sure I can't offer you *anything*—? Maybe a small glass of wine?

GREGOR. No. Really. Thank you.

HARRIET. Besides, we've intruded enough on you, already. . . . (*Pauses curiously as a bright flashing yellow light—apparently from the street below—is seen in the area near the window.*) Oh! Alex, isn't that for *you*—?

ALEX. (*Sees light.*) Hey, yeah! I'd better get downstairs, quick! (*Only gets one step toward door when* GRACE *grabs his arm.*)

GRACE. (*Who has completely misinterpreted source of light.*) Oh, Alex, don't! I can't have them lock you up! You mustn't give in without a fight!

GREGOR. Is something wrong—?

ALEX. (*Trying to keep the non-existent cat inside the bag.*) Grace, honey, it's only a pickup truck, I had a little engine trouble—!

GRACE. What? Oh, thank heaven! I thought it was the police!

HARRIET. Why should the *police* be after *Alex?*

GRACE. (*Meaning* ALEX *isn't a foolproof burglar.*) Well, *nobody's perfect—!*

GREGOR. (*Only means he doesn't follow the conversation.*) I beg your pardon—?

GRACE. (*Thinking she's insulted him.*) Oh, present company excepted, of course!

ALEX. (*Who doesn't know what* GREGOR *does.*) How's that again?

GRACE. (*Now thinks she's insulted* him.) Oh, darling, I didn't mean you, you're an absolutely *perfect* burglar!

ALEX. (*The jig is up.*) Oh-boy!

GREGOR. Alex? My fiancee's brother-in-law?

HARRIET. A burglar?

GRACE. (*Now hopelessly confused.*) *I* thought you *knew—?!*

GREGOR. Harriet, is this true—?

HARRIET. It can't be! He told me he worked for the telephone company!

GRACE. (*Pleased.*) Oh, Alex, how clever of you!

HARRIET. Grace—you mean—he *is* a burglar?!

GRACE. (*Points with pride toward vacant tabletop.*) He just stole an entire silver service!

HARRIET. (*Notices its absence for first time, wails.*) Aaaaah! I've been robbed!

GRACE. (*Not connecting her with silver service.*) You, *too?!* . . . Alex, how *could* you?! . . . Harriet, what did he take?

HARRIET. That silver service! It was right there on the table! What's he done with it?

GRACE. But Harriet—*I* took *that—*

HARRIET. You're in this thing *together?!*

GREGOR. (*Who has been sadly but firmly moving toward door.*) Harriet—under the circumstances—I think it might be better all around if—

ALEX. You're not leaving? Listen, I can explain—

GREGOR. (*Puts a hand upon his shoulder.*) No need,

no need. Old Russian Proverb: "No matter how warm the smile on the face of the sun, the cat still has her kittens under the porch!" (*Exits, shutting door after him; others stand staring blankly out front for three full beats; then:*)

ALEX. (*Starts for door.*) I'll *stop* him—!

GRACE. (*Grabs his arm.*) No, don't! Haven't you murdered *enough* people for one night?!

HARRIET. (*Backing from him in horror.*) He *murdered* someone?

GRACE. For that silver service.

HARRIET. (*At sea.*) But that was *Mother's* . . . *!?*

GRACE. Alex! You murdered *Mother?!*

ALEX. Of course not! . . . Now, listen, there's something I've *got* to clear up right *now!*

GRACE. No, wait, there's something *I've* got to clear up *first!* (*Turns to* HARRIET.) I want you to know something. I don't *care* what Gregor Vanitzky thinks! The only reason Alex is here is because he *is* a burglar! I want to help straighten him out, because then I feel I can maybe let myself *love* him! Why, if Alex weren't a criminal, I'd never look twice at him! (ALEX *reacts, now must do some heavy thinking, as she turns to him.*) Now, what did *you* want to clear up?

ALEX. (*After about three beats recites like schoolboy.*) I first decided on a life of crime at age ten. Ah, how well I remember my first caper . . . ! It was a candy store. . . .

(*And as the two women stare at him with sudden hope for him—*)

THE CURTAIN FALLS

ACT THREE

It is about two hours later. ALEX'S *jacket,* HARRIET'S *suitcase, and the cap pistol are no longer in the room. At curtain-rise, we find* GRACE, HARRIET *and* ALEX *seated at the table, a bottle of bourbon on the table, and half-finished bourbons-on-the-rocks in glasses before them.* ALEX *is Upstage,* HARRIET *Left, and* GRACE *Right.* HARRIET *is now in a nightgown, robe and slippers, and* GRACE *now wears a nightgown beneath her robe. All three are slightly fuzzy from drinking. The Christmas tree is just where it was, untouched in all its one-sided splendor of ornaments. The window is dark, the flashing light no longer operating.* HARRIET *is speaking as scene begins.*

HARRIET. . . . and *another* thing—if Gregor Vanitzky had even one little *tenth* of the charity and love he is always so busy *preaching* at people, he would have gone ahead and married me *anyhow,* burglar or *no* burglar—!

ALEX and GRACE. (*In unison, apparently part of an already-established pattern of behavior during the drinking bout, raise their glasses on:*) Right on!

(*Solemnly take large swallows of their drinks, then clunk glasses back onto tabletop, and* ALEX *and* GRACE *listen, with the over-intensity of the slightly pie-eyed, to:*)

HARRIET. . . . and *another* thing—if he was willing to marry me for better or worse *after* marriage, the *least* he could do is marry me for better or worse *before—!*

ALEX and GRACE. (*Same business.*) Right on! (*Both drink, clunk glasses to table;* HARRIET *sits silent.*)

GRACE. (*After a moment.*) Alex. Shouldn't you go downstairs and talk to the man with the repair truck?

ALEX. Grace. I did. Hours and hours ago.

HARRIET. (*Although they pay no attention, does glass-raise on:*) Right on! (*Drinks, clunks glass to table, unnoticed.*)

GRACE. Alex. Are you sure?

ALEX. Of course I am sure. You even made a joke about it. You said if only the man knew he was unfreezing the gas-line on a notorious getaway car.

GRACE. *I* said that?

ALEX. You most certainly did.

GRACE. Did we all laugh?

ALEX. Until our sides hurt.

GRACE. Good.

HARRIET. (*Same business.*) Right on! (*This time, they look at her as she drinks and clunks down the glass; about one post-clunk beat later, she senses their stares, straightens, and decides to speak.*) Know something? Being a burglar is not so bad.

ALEX. (*Nods solemnly, quotes:*) "Who steals my purse, steals trash!"

GRACE. I didn't know you carried a purse.

ALEX. Well, now you know.

GRACE. Then where is it?

ALEX. I just told you, somebody stole it. Weren't you paying attention?

GRACE. I forgive you.

ALEX. That's all right.

HARRIET. (*As though she had not already said so.*) Know something? Being a burglar is not so bad.

GRACE. Not if you are a success at it. (*Abruptly snorts and giggles at her own remark; the other two just stare blearily at her; after a bit, she quiets.*) Forgive me. I am not accustomed to drinking bourbon at this hour. In fact, I am not accustomed to drinking bourbon.

ALEX. (*Gallantly.*) I would never have guessed it.

HARRIET. Neither am I.

ALEX. Well, I did guess that.

HARRIET. How?

ALEX. You bend your head forward instead of tilting the glass back. That's why your nose is so wet.

GRACE. Harriet?

HARRIET. Yes?

GRACE. *Why* is being a burglar not so bad?

HARRIET. Because there are other crimes much worse. Take Gregor.

ALEX. I do not want Gregor.

HARRIET. Take him anyway.

ALEX. (*Shrugs, gives in with a nod.*) Got him.

HARRIET. Grace?

GRACE. Got him.

HARRIET. Take Gregor: He is worse than a burglar. A burglar steals trashy purses. (*Sobs:*) Gregor stole my heart.

ALEX and GRACE. (*Same business.*) Right on! (*Drink/ clunk, callously, while she sobs miserably.*)

GRACE. Take the telephone company. It steals people's dimes.

ALEX. I resent that. I don't *deny* it, but I *resent* it!

GRACE and HARRIET. Why?

ALEX. (*Even snockered, remembers his apparent occupation.*) No special reason. (*Lifts bottle to quickly change subject.*) Would anybody like some more? (GRACE and HARRIET *will each extend glass on individual line:*)

GRACE. I think I've had enough.

HARRIET. I *know* I've had enough.

ALEX. (*Refills their glasses, and then, while refilling his own:*) I like women who can hold their liquor.

GRACE and HARRIET. (*Same business.*) Right on!

ALEX. Well, what do you say, am I reformed yet?

GRACE. I am not sure. I am very new at reforming people.

HARRIET. You have to start somewhere.

GRACE. That's true.

ALEX. Just how long does this reformation take? How long must I sit here?

GRACE. Until I am convinced you will never burgle again.

HARRIET. I hope he is in a comfortable chair.

ALEX. I would rather be in a comfortable bed.

HARRIET. You newlyweds are all alike. (*When they both stare at her, a little sobered—only a very little sobered—by this reminder, and then stare at each other.*) Do not tell me you have *forgotten*—?

ALEX. Well. As a matter of fact—

GRACE. —there is something you should know, Harriet. (*Rises.*)

HARRIET. Is it about Gregor?

ALEX. No. (*Then, to* GRACE, *as an afterthought.*) At least, I do not think so.

GRACE. No, it is not about Gregor.

HARRIET. Then go ahead.

GRACE. (*Stares at her a moment; then:*) What was I going to say?

ALEX. I don't remember.

HARRIET. Neither do I.

GRACE. Then it couldn't have been important. (*Sits.*)

ALEX and HARRIET. (*Same business.*) Right on! (*Drink/ clunk.*)

GRACE. Wait— I remember! I have a very important decision to make. About *me*, and Alex, and Walter! . . . Harriet, there is something you should know—!

HARRIET. (*Blurrily.*) Grace—did we have this conversation before?

GRACE. Only half of it. I forgot to *tell* you the something.

HARRIET. Will it upset me?

GRACE. (*Guiltily.*) Uh-huh.

HARRIET. Then don't tell me. I've had enough upsets tonight—my brother-in-law is a burglar, my fiance is a fink—!

GRACE. Never mind that. The point is, should I marry *Walter* or *Alex?!*

ALEX. Grace, you haven't been *asked* . . . (*She looks at him, and he finishes:*) yet.

GRACE. Well . . . whenever! (*Returns gaze to HAR-RIET, during:*)

ALEX. Grace—don't tell me you are even *considering* marrying *Walter?*

GRACE. But I've known him *such* a long time—and he *is* a nice *man*—and he can offer me such wonderful things! Like . . . *security—!* (*Ticks Item One off on little finger, then cannot think of Item Two; three beats; then:*)

HARRIET. (*Fighting her way through the fuzziness.*) Grace . . . how can you marry Walter if you're married to Alex?

GRACE. (*Stands suddenly—not quite steadily, but suddenly.*) I am *not* married to *Alex!*

ALEX. (*Not to be outdone, stands in similar sudden-unsteady manner.*) And *Grace* is not married to *me!*

GRACE. I just *said* that.

ALEX. Oh.

HARRIET. Then why are we having this party?

GRACE. This was to celebrate Alex's reformation from burglary. Have you so soon forgotten?

ALEX. Hey, how did I make out? Am I all rehabilitated, or what?

GRACE. Of course you are. You promised.

ALEX. What did I promise?

GRACE. (*Will tick items off on her fingers as she names them.*) First—you will never go a-burgling again . . .

ALEX. (*Remembering.*) Oh, yeah.

GRACE. Second—you will return every last one of your ill-gotten gains . . .

ALEX. (*Similarly.*) Oh, yeah.

GRACE. And finally—most important of all—you will stop making phone calls to Marge!

ALEX. (*Surprised he made* this *promise.*) Oh! Yeah?

HARRIET. Grace, you are jealous.

GRACE. Well, what wife would *not* be?

HARRIET. But you are not a wife.

GRACE. I will be, after Walter gets here.

ALEX. You are going to marry *Walter?!*

GRACE. I don't know. But I can't make up my mind until he's here. He should be back any minute.

HARRIET. Grace, how can you be sure Walter will *ever* come back?

(*There is a KNOCK at the door; all look that way a moment, then return gazes where they were; no one moves to door.*)

GRACE. I just have a premonition. (*KNOCK repeats.*)

HARRIET. Isn't one of you going to answer the door? (*Looks from one to the other; both are supporting themselves with hands flat upon the table and swaying slightly.*)

ALEX. I'm not sure I can get here from there.

HARRIET. Grace?

GRACE. I'll be happy to go, just as soon as this room settles down. (*KNOCK repeats, a bit more urgently.*)

HARRIET. Oh, all right, *I'll* go! (*With solemn dignity, she proceeds to door opens door and* WALTER *enters; his homburg is in both hands at stomach-height, his manner forlorn and subdued; he will walk unhappily to* HAR-RIET'S *vacated chair, sit there, and place his homburg on the table before him, and stare at it, never raising his eyes from it until indicated.* HARRIET *closes door, but remains there, swaying unsteadily.*)

GRACE. (*As soon as he is in position at table.*) Walter. I knew you'd come back.

WALTER. (*Not even hearing her.*) I've never felt so miserable in my entire life.

HARRIET. (*Hand to stomach, knows she is going to be*

sick.) I know what you *mean—! (Exits fast, to bath-room, on:)* Excuse me . . . !

ALEX. You didn't enjoy your party?

WALTER. It *wasn't* my party. I only thought it was.

GRACE. Then whose party was it?

WALTER. The chairman's!

ALEX. But—I thought the chairman was coming to the party to shake your hand.

WALTER. I misunderstood Lydia on the phone. She said something about shaking hands with the chairman, and I naturally assumed *he* was supposed to come there to shake hands with *me,* not the other way around.

GRACE. But—didn't Lydia say she was giving a party for your birthday—?

WALTER. No. She said I was invited to celebrate the happy occasion, and I just assumed *that* was the occasion she *meant.*

ALEX. Then—what *was* the occasion?

WALTER. (*Finally raises his woebegone face to look at* ALEX.) It was an engagement party. He's going to marry Lydia!

GRACE. (*Sobered with sympathy.*) Oh, *Walter . . . !*

WALTER. (*Staring at his homburg once more.*) I've never been so horribly embarrassed. All evening long, before the chairman showed up, I kept going around *thanking* people for coming. No *wonder* they were look-ing at me so strangely!

GRACE. Oh, Walter, how *terrible* for you!

WALTER. I haven't come to the worst part.

ALEX. (*Semi-sobered with sympathy.*) How could it get any worse?

WALTER. Easy. The chairman finally showed up. In order to commemorate the occasion, I started taking movies of his entrance into Lydia's home, and then I went forward to shake his hand. I was happily waiting for him to say "Happy Birthday," when somebody said, "Hey, let's get the presents!" While I was trying to look

shy and unworthy, everybody walked right *past* me! And
there they all were, congratulating the chairman, congratulating Lydia, and handing them both gift after gift
after gift . . . ! (HARRIET *re-enters, looking better, now
starts for door.*)

GRACE. Oh, Walter! And you didn't *have* one for them!

WALTER. I know. And they were looking at me, ex-
pectantly . . . !

ALEX. What the hell did you do?

WALTER. Only one thing I *could* do. . . . I gave him
my brand-new Super-8 movie camera! (HARRIET *closes
door; distracted by the sound, the others turn.*)

GRACE. Harriet, where have you *been?*

HARRIET. Sorry. Something came up.

(*Satisfied, the others return to their prior positions, and
as* HARRIET *makes her less-wobbly way to a point
just Upstage of* WALTER'S *chair—the back of which
she will use for support with her left hand—*WALTER
sorrowfully returns to his story.)

WALTER. The chairman was very pleased. He said it
was the best present he'd ever gotten.

ALEX. Was Lydia pleased?

WALTER. I'm not sure. She told me I should have
wrapped it.

GRACE. Probably just jealous because he liked your
present better than hers.

ALEX. What *was* Lydia's present to the chairman?

WALTER. Lydia.

HARRIET. Excuse me— (*When they all look her way.*)
Who is Lydia?

WALTER. (*Stands suddenly and faces away from her,
Downstage.*) I don't want to talk about it anymore.

GRACE. Of course you don't, you poor dear! Here, give
me your things—! (*Will manage to get to him and get
his hat and overcoat.*)

WALTER. Thank you. Would you have a drink—?

GRACE. No thanks, I've had too much already.

WALTER. I mean for me.

HARRIET. (*Still supporting herself on chair, gestures with free hand.*) Take mine. I don't want to overdo it. (WALTER *sits again, and as* GRACE *makes her way off through curtains with his things, picks up* HARRIET'S *drink.*)

WALTER. Thanks, Harriet. (*Takes a good swallow, catches his breath; the drink seems to have restored him a bit as he abruptly re-resumes:*) But let me get to the *worst* part—

ALEX. (*Drops back into his chair in disbelief.*) You mean you *haven't?*

WALTER. Wait'll you *hear—! (Will sip at, and finally finish,* HARRIET'S *drink, during:*) I quickly explained to Lydia that it wasn't wrapped because I also was making them a present of the films of their engagement party— (*Sip.*) but then on the way back here I remembered that there's some *other* footage on that reel!

ALEX. (*As* GRACE *re-enters.*) What kind of footage?

WALTER. Footage of the *chairman* at our convention in *Miami, body*-painting a *blonde* in a blue *bikini! (Drains entire remainder of drink.*)

GRACE. Oh, is *that* all! (*When her dismissive tone makes the others stare at her.*) I thought you were going to say you had footage of *me* in that *hula* outfit and *Alex* in his *underwear!*

WALTER. (*His eyes go wide, his jaw drops, and he stands, horrified.*) Ye gods! I *have! (To* GRACE.) And Lydia knows you're my secretary!

GRACE. (*Shocked almost to tears.*) But that means— I could lose my job!

WALTER. (*Lurches into her arms, sobs aloud:*) Welcome to the club!

HARRIET. Oh, poor Walter! What are you going to do?!

WALTER. I have no idea. It's hopeless. I *can't* just break into Lydia's place and *steal* it back! If only I were on good terms with a professional burglar. (GRACE, HARRIET *and* ALEX *react simultaneously, though of course not in the same manner; the women are aglow with delight,* ALEX *is ashen with ghastly apprehension;* WALTER *notices the charged atmosphere, looks about in puzzlement.*) What is it? Why does everybody look so funny?

GRACE. Alex—?

ALEX. (*Rises slowly from his chair, completely sobered by panic.*) Now—wait a minute—hold on—Grace—!

GRACE. But you *heard* what Walter said—?!

ALEX. Yeah! He said on *good terms* with a burglar. Since when have *I* been on good terms with *Walter?*

WALTER. Since when have you been a *burglar?*

HARRIET. Oh, *all along*, Walter! Isn't it exciting?

WALTER. But *he* told me he was with the *telephone* company!

GRACE. Of course he did! (*With adoring glance at* ALEX.) That's his M.O.!

WALTER. Come to think of it—he *didn't* show me his identification—!

ALEX. Well, I will *now!* (*Fumbles at pockets.*) I must have left it in my jacket—! (*Takes step toward bedroom, but* GRACE *springs up and stops him, her hands gently upon his chest.*)

GRACE. Alex! I know how you feel about Walter—but —even if you wouldn't do it for him—won't you do it for me?

ALEX. But I can't! I don't know how to burgle! I mean, I'm terrible at it! I always make mistakes—! (*But he stops because* GRACE *is now kissing him; then, when she is done:*) I'll get caught!

WALTER. (*After observing them for a moment.*) I'll take that risk!

GRACE. (*As she and* ALEX *break from clinch.*) Well, Alex—what do you say?

WALTER. (*Staring glumly into space, speaks almost to himself.*) What *can* he say? What could *any* man say? If she kissed *me* like that, *I'd* go burgle the place! (*Sits.*)

ALEX. (*Grasping at straws.*) Grace, did you hear *that?! Walter's* willing to do it! All you have to do is kiss him! Isn't that great?! (WALTER *brightens, then dims on:*)

HARRIET. But Walter's no good at it. Walter might get caught.

ALEX. Yeah, but—but— Look, what about my *reformation,* for pete's sake?! You made me promise, on my solemn oath, that I'd never burgle again!

GRACE. But this is an emergency!

HARRIET. And it wouldn't *really* be stealing . . . after all, it *is* Walter's camera!

ALEX. But look—hey—listen—I—Grace, I haven't even *cased* the joint!

WALTER. (*With energy from rekindled hope, springs up.*) Don't worry! I've been there! I'll draw you a map!

ALEX. (*Dully.*) Thanks a heap.

HARRIET. Good, then it's all settled!

ALEX. The *hell* it is! I'm not risking my neck to save Walter's!

GRACE. But what about mine? When Lydia sees me in that Hawaiian outfit—!

ALEX. What does that matter? You'll have *me* to support you!

GRACE. *How?* You haven't even got a *job!*

ALEX. So I'll *get* one! I've been playing telephone man so long, it should be a *snap* to start doing it legitimately—!

GRACE. Oh, Alex—*could* you?!

ALEX. For you—*anything!*

GRACE. Then, you'll burgle Walter's camera back—?!

ALEX. (*Sunk.*) What the hell. Why not!

WALTER. I'll draw you that map—!

ALEX. I won't need it. Just the address.

HARRIET and WALTER. *Really . . . ?!*

ALEX. (*Contriving it as he goes along.*) Should be a snap, far as I can see. I knock on the door, tell her there's been trouble reported with her telephone, she lets me in, I keep an eye out for the camera, pop it into my tool kit, tell her the phone's okay, and head back here with the loot! (*Shrugs helplessly, starts toward curtains again.*)

GRACE. Oh, you marvelous man! You make it sound so easy!

ALEX. (*Pauses just short of exit, says sincerely:*) You wanta know something? I think it *will* be!

WALTER. Even easier than you think! Lydia stashed all the presents on the bed, and there's a phone on the bedside table!

HARRIET. Isn't it wonderful to have a foolproof M.O.!

ALEX. (*Gives her an incredulous look, then exits to bedroom, on:*) Where's my jacket—?

GRACE. (*A split second later.*) Oh! (*Dashes off after him.*) Alex, wait! You'll never find it in the dark!

HARRIET. I still haven't figured out why she doesn't want Alex to know she has a television set . . .

WALTER. (*With a patient teacher-to-pupil tone.*) Harriet, television sets cost *money,* and the man is a *burglar!* (*Shrugs.*) Seems perfectly clear to *me* . . .

HARRIET. (*Sinks into* ALEX's *vacated chair, blinking in confusion.*) I never thought of that . . . (*She and* WALTER *look up as* ALEX *and* GRACE *re-enter; he is in his jacket and carrying his tool kit, she has her cloth coat on over her nightgown.*)

WALTER. Grace! Where are *you* going?

GRACE. *Somebody* has to show him the way to Lydia's —and who's going to drive the getaway car?

ALEX. Truck.

GRACE. Truck.

WALTER. But *I* could show him the way—

HARRIET. (*Stops his half-rise from his chair with her hand on his arm.*) Walter, are you nuts? Why, if Lydia sees *you*—

ALEX. (*As he and* GRACE *continue moving toward door.*) I'm afraid Harriet's right, Walter. We can't take any chances.

WALTER. (*Still-half-risen.*) Wait—I don't understand—

HARRIET. (*And as she speaks, an awed* WALTER *will stare in amazement at her and slowly sink back into his chair, while* ALEX *and* GRACE—*similarly impressed—will pause at half-open door.*) Listen, kiddo, you're the joe who set up this caper, and if the patsy gets a good glom at your mug, she's gonna buzz the fuzz, and you'll wind up doing ten-to-twenty in the slammer!

WALTER. (*After a silence.*) Now I understand.

ALEX. Good. (*He and* GRACE *exit, closing door after them.*)

WALTER. Harriet—where in the world did you pick up that kind of talk?

HARRIET. *Sesame Street.*

WALTER. (*Absorbs this, then reaches for bottle.*) I need another drink.

HARRIET. (*Stops him.*) No you don't! What you need is a square meal!

WALTER. So *fix* me something!

HARRIET. Grace hasn't got anything but cornflakes and milk. She wasn't expecting all this company.

WALTER. Damn. I'm starving! I was so upset at Lydia's party I didn't even have any hors d'oeuvres! . . . (*Looks at her in sudden decision.*) Let's go out!

HARRIET. Walter—do you mean it?

WALTER. Of course I mean it! I'm starved—you're starved—and we'll both probably spend the rest of our lives in jail, anyhow—!

HARRIET. You've got a date! (*Bolts for bedroom.*) I'll be dressed and ready in three minutes! (*Exits through curtains.*)

WALTER. (*Calls after her.*) Bring my coat and hat when you come back—! (*Stands, smooths his suit, adjusts his tie, palm-brushes his hair back at the temples, and we can see he is beginning to feel peppy and dapper; then*

*there is a KNOCK at the door; surprised—and a bit
nervous—he goes to it, queries softly:*) Who is it—?

GREGOR. (*Off.*) Gregor Vanitzky!

WALTER. (*Amazed at the name.*) *Greg*or Van-
itzky . . . ?! I don't believe it.

GREGOR. (*Off.*) Nevertheless, it is I! (*Enters as a
curious WALTER reluctantly opens the door.*) I can understand your surprise, after the way I walked out of here—
(*Sees WALTER, realizes he is a stranger.*) Oh. I don't believe we've met . . . ?

WALTER. No, we haven't. I'm Walter Chepple. (GREGOR
does Prussian heel-click; fascinated, WALTER echoes:)
Walter Chepple. (GREGOR *does it again; WALTER lets it
drop, goes on:*) Can I help you—? (*Will shut door as
GREGOR moves farther into room.*)

GREGOR. I was hoping to find Miss Larkin at home.

WALTER. Oh, well, she—uh—she had to go out for a
little while.

GREGOR. Will she be back soon?

WALTER. (*Sincere prayer heavenward for GRACE's
safety.*) If God is good!

GREGOR. (*Beat.*) He is. (*Beat.*) I'll wait. (*Undoes
front of overcoat, but does not remove it.*) I suppose she's
told you about me—or has she?

WALTER. I'm sorry, no. What was it you wished to see
her about? . . . No, wait, that's none of my business.

GREGOR. Oh, there's nothing secret about it. I have
simply decided to go ahead with the wedding.

WALTER. What wedding? You don't mean—Miss
Larkin—?

GREGOR. I know it must surprise you, considering my
occupation—

WALTER. Excuse me, but—what *is* your occupation—?

GREGOR. Why, I'm a minister of the gospel. That's
why I was so upset, earlier, when I learned what Alex
did for a living—oh, but perhaps *you* don't know about
Alex! Oh, dear, I hope I haven't spilled the borscht—?

WALTER. Well—uh—that's hard for me to say . . . I mean, *I* know what he does, but I still can't be sure *you* know the same thing *I* do, so— Let me put it this way—does his job begin with a "B"—?

GREGOR. (*Sighs with relief.*) Ah, good, then you *do* know! Yes, I'm well aware of his less-than-honest activities, but—I got to thinking—if all men are to live as brothers, we must make allowances for one another's weaknesses! So I have returned in full willingness to go through with the ceremony.

WALTER. Grace sure doesn't waste any time! She barely *knows* the guy! How did she dig *you* up so fast?

GREGOR. Just a moment—I'm afraid I did not quite follow that . . . ?

WALTER. Listen, I appreciate your trying to make it easy on me, but that's all right. I knew I'd lost her when I saw her persuade him to go out on this one last job—

GREGOR. You mean—Alex is out committing burglary right *now*—?

WALTER. Well, yes, but only as a special favor to *me*.

GREGOR. What are *you*, his *manager?!*

WALTER. Don't be ridiculous! I'm in the insurance business!

GREGOR. I might have guessed!

WALTER. And just what is *that* supposed to mean?!

GREGOR. Well, after all, your occupation and Alex's are not that dissimilar! He's into *burglary*, you're running a *protection* racket!

WALTER. Now, just one minute—

GREGOR. When an insurance agent is making a sale, does he not stress all the potential hazards the prospect faces? Car accidents, sudden death, and the like?

WALTER. Well, yes, but—

GREGOR. But who *qualifies* for a policy? . . . Only those people that the insurance company is satisfied are not *likely* to have car accidents or die without warning!

WALTER. Well, yes, but—

GREGOR. And don't the agents tell the prospects that the company is interested *only* in protecting the prospect's *future?*

WALTER. Uh . . . well, sure . . .

GREGOR. But before they'll sign him, they make a complete investigation of the prospect's *past!*

WALTER. Well, they *have* to, because . . . because . . .

GREGOR. I think we can sum the whole thing up in one sentence: The only people an insurance company will *protect* are those people who are never going to make a *claim!*

WALTER. That's—that's just good *business!*

GREGOR. Which *also* begins with a "B"!

(*As* WALTER *tries to think of a reply,* HARRIET *enters from bedroom; she is dressed again, and in her overcoat, and is carrying* WALTER'S *overcoat and homburg; she sees* GREGOR *and stops, surprised, just inside room.*)

HARRIET. Why, Gregor! It's you!

GREGOR. Harriet! (*To* WALTER.) I thought you told me she'd gone out?

WALTER. That she—? Wait a minute, is *this* the Miss Larkin you said you were coming here to marry?

GREGOR. Of course it is!

WALTER. But—marry her to *who?*

GREGOR. To *me!*

WALTER. (*Imagining a minister officiating at his own wedding.*) Can he *do* that?

HARRIET. Of course he can't, Walter!

GREGOR. (*Comprehending* WALTER'S *confusion.*) No-no, Mister Chepple, you *misunderstood.* Naturally, Harriet and I will have *another* minister witness our marriage.

HARRIET. No-no, Gregor, *you* misunderstood. I say,

"Of course you can't," because *I* wouldn't have you if you came with *chocolate sprinkles! (Starts helping a surprised-but-pleased* WALTER *into his overcoat.*) Let's get out of here, Walter. I'm ready to faint from hunger!

GREGOR. Harriet, you can't *mean* this! After all we've been to each other—all our plans and hopes—to go off this way just because of one little argument—!

HARRIET. But it *wasn't* a *little* argument, Gregor. It was a real eye-opener. It wasn't just your intolerance for human frailty, or your surprisingly unforgiving attitude, or your walking out without even giving me a chance to explain or apologize—

GREGOR. Then—what *was* it? What *happened?*

HARRIET. Nothing. Nothing at all. That's just the point. You walked right out of my life—and I didn't feel a thing. Except, maybe—relief.

WALTER. Harriet, what are you saying?

HARRIET. I had no idea I was uptight about marrying Gregor until he walked out, and then I felt so good, I started thinking— Did I really want to spend the rest of my life polishing a halo? Never taking another drink, never sneaking a smoke, never learning to *Hustle—!*

GREGOR and WALTER. *Harriet!*

HARRIET. I mean the *dance!* That's when I knew that if I married Gregor, I'd end up living in sin!

GREGOR. *Living* in *sin?!*

HARRIET. Isn't lying a sin? Gregor, if I married you, and pretended I didn't want to do all those things, I'd be living a *lie.* And what kind of a preacher's wife would *that* make me?! (*Gently and briefly takes his hand.*) I'm sorry, Gregor, but it just wouldn't work. (*Drops his hand, turns to* WALTER.) Well, shall we go?

GREGOR. (*Folds his arms.*) Nevertheless, Harriet, I refuse to believe this is the end. Sooner or later, you will see the error of your ways. And when that day comes, no matter how long it takes, I want you to know: I Gregor, will be waiting.

HARRIET. (*Now at door with* WALTER, *who has his hand on the knob.*) Now, really, Gregor! You don't *mean* that. Why, I'll bet the next pretty convert you meet—

GREGOR. (*Solemnly raises his right hand, and intones ringingly:*) Harriet Larkin! I tell you, here and now, that if I speak anything other than the absolute truth, may heaven strike me down where I stand! (*And the Christmas tree topples forward to the floor with a shattering crash; as a shaken* GREGOR *stares at this near-miss,* HARRIET *raises her eyes to heaven and says quietly:*)

HARRIET. You missed.

WALTER. (*Same heavenward-gaze business.*) How about two out of three—?!

GREGOR. (*Still slightly in shock.*) Old Russian Proverb: "When the mist moves into Minsk, the wise man keeps his sleeve out of the soup!" (*Exits.*)

WALTER. Soup! That reminds me, Harriet—! (*At this moment,* ALEX *and* GRACE *burst happily in through the door.*)

ALEX. Walter, you're saved!

GRACE. (*Hands something to* WALTER.) Look what Alex found on the front seat of your car!

HARRIET. Walter, what is it?

WALTER. The film!

GRACE. It must have fallen out before you ever *got* to Lydia's!

WALTER. But—how did you—?

ALEX. You left your headlights on again. I went to your car to turn them off, opened the front door, the dome light came on—and there it was!

HARRIET. Oh, but what will the chairman say when he finds there isn't any film in your camera?

WALTER. He'll think *Lydia* lost it! (*All cheer.*)

HARRIET. (*Rushing into his arms as* GRACE *rushes into*

ALEX'S.) Oh, Walter, I'm so happy for you! (*Hugs him warmly.*)

WALTER. (*Returns the hug.*) Thank you. Harriet— you're quite a woman—!

ALEX. (*As he and* GRACE *look in surprise at the embracing couple.*) Did we miss something?

WALTER. No, but *I* almost did. (*Looks fondly at* HARRIET.) I'm awfully glad I didn't.

HARRIET. Me, too, Walter. Me, too. (*Then she briskly breaks embrace.*) Well! Walter and I were just going out for some dinner. Join us?

GRACE. (*Who, of course, still wears her nightgown beneath her coat.*) That's a wonderful idea. But I can't go like this—let me change out of my nightgown, and Alex and I will catch up with you! (*Starts for bedroom, but stops on:*)

WALTER. Where shall we go?

GRACE. Oh, there's a very nice little Italian place, right near the corner of 69th and Roosevelt. It's only a block or so.

WALTER. (*To* HARRIET.) You *like* Italian food—?

HARRIET. *Molto bene!*

WALTER. (*Happily.*) *Mama mia!* (*Links his arm in hers, and they exit to hall, on:*)

HARRIET. (*Waving gaily at others.*) *Arrivederci!*

GRACE. (*Calls after them.*) Oh, and *thanks* for taking down the *tree!* (*Shuts the door behind them; she almost exits to bedroom, then hesitates, her manner somewhat abashed and shy; she seems unhappy about something;* ALEX, *after a moment, senses her mood and stares; she manages a faint little smile, and when he continues to stare at her in curiosity, she finds her voice, somehow, and speaks.*) Alex . . . there's something you should know . . .

ALEX. (*Looking at her, and loving her.*) What, honey . . . ?

GRACE. Well . . . as long as I'm making *you* turn honest . . . because I *do* think honesty is a very important quality . . . especially between two people . . . *I* have to be completely honest with *you* . . .

ALEX. Grace . . . you don't have to tell me anything you don't want to—

GRACE. Oh, but I *do* want to! I mean, if you and I get married, sooner or later I'm going to have to break down and tell you—

ALEX. Tell me what?

GRACE. (*Her eyes filling with tears as she declares:*) I have a seventeen-inch color portable at the bottom of my wardrobe! (*Her hands suddenly cover her face, and she turns away.*)

ALEX. Aw, you poor baby! (*Goes to her, turns her tenderly toward him, holds her as she weeps miserably against his chest.*) No wonder you panicked every time I started in there!

GRACE. (*Barely intelligible as she speaks between sobs against him.*) I'm a regular television *freak!* I almost *never* stop watching! I watch game shows, soap operas, kiddie cartoons, and every one of the network movies—! (*Pulls her head back so she can look up into his face and wail:*) I don't have *any* mind at *all!* (*Re-buries her face against his chest, shaking with sobs.*)

ALEX. Now, wait—wait just a minute here—maybe— you might feel better if I told you—I haven't exactly been a pillar of veracity myself . . . (*Her sobs quiet a bit, and she peeps tearfully up at him.*)

GRACE. What do you mean?

ALEX. Well—I hate to destroy your illusions about me, but—Grace, honey, *I'm* not a burglar. Never *have* been. I just pretended to be, because you were so intent on reforming me, it seemed like a good idea to make you keep me around!

GRACE. (*Delighted.*) Oh, Alex! (*Hugs him hard, her face again upon his chest; then, in a moment, she leans back and looks up at him in puzzlement.*) But—if you're not a burglar—what *are* you?

ALEX. I'm just a simple, ordinary, everyday *line* man!

GRACE. (*Eyes widening along with her radiant smile.*) But—that's marvelous! If there's one thing I'm really *bananas* about, it's *football* players! (*Happily pillows her cheek against his chest, as the CURTAIN begins a slow and romantic descent.*)

ALEX. (*Smiles helplessly, stares unseeingly out front, absently starts stroking* GRACE'S *hair with his Upstage hand, as they maintain their cozy embrace, during:*) You're *so* intelligent . . . so *very* intelligent . . . so *incredibly* intelligent! (*And, by now, of course—*)

THE CURTAIN IS DOWN

(*Alternative ending used in premiere production, replacing* ALEX'S *curtain-line, above:*)

ALEX. (*Smiles fondly at her.*) Say goodnight, Gracie.
GRACE. (*Smiles at audience.*) Goodnight.

THE CURTAIN FALLS

PROPERTY LIST

PRESET AT TOP OF SHOW—
In Cabinet:
pots, pans, dustpan, flashlight, whisk broom
In Hutch:
cups, saucers, glasses, cutlery
On Counter:
various bottles and jars, including a bottle each of wine
whiskey, roll of paper towels
On Table:
coffee cup, saucer, cereal bowl, spoon, Corn Flakes box
On Refrigerator:
pantyhose draped from coils to dry
In Refrigerator:
tray of ice cubes
On Christmas Tree:
ornaments on Downstage side only, and one easily detach-
able (and replaceable) branch

ACT ONE:
CARRIED ON BY—
GRACE:
cap pistol, with spiral roll of caps in it
WALTER:
business card in suit pocket, Super-8 movie camera
ALEX:
tool kit containing large wrench, piece of paper containing
"G. Larkin"and address in jacket pocket
HARRIET:
large suitcase which—when opened in next Act—will con-
tain cloth-wrapped silver service atop usual suitcase items
dresses, shoes, whatever)

ACT TWO:
CARRIED ON BY—
GRACE:
large empty cardboard carton (corrugated type), Harriet's
suitcase from bedroom

90

ACT THREE:

CLEAR—

> suitcase, cap pistol, move Alex's jacket and tool kit into Offstage bedoom area

PRESET—

> 3 glasses with ice and bourbon in them on table, bottle of bourbon (about two-thirds full) on table

CARRIED ON BY—

> GRACE:

> film cassette suitable for Super-8 movie camera

SOUND EFFECTS

Doors knocks; clanking and hacking of tools outside window; loud gush of water outside window; phone bell; crash (*of falling* WALTER) in bedroom; pop (*of breaking light bulb*) in bedroom

LIGHT EFFECTS

Flashing yellow light outside window in Act Two

Recommendation: Hang a lot of metal bells on tree, so sound is as funny as sight, when it nearly clobbers Gregor. Ornaments, of course, should be unbreakable.

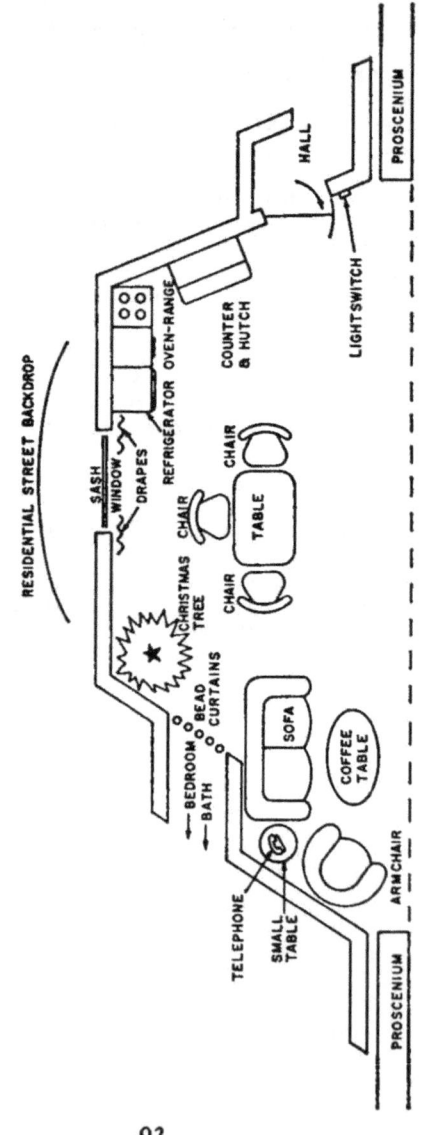

STAGE PLAN
FOR
"SAVING GRACE"

RESIDENTIAL STREET BACKDROP

SASH
WINDOW
DRAPES

REFRIGERATOR OVEN-RANGE

COUNTER
& HUTCH

HALL

LIGHT SWITCH

PROSCENIUM

CHAIR

CHAIR

TABLE

CHAIR

CHRISTMAS
TREE

BEDROOM
BATH

BEAD
CURTAINS

SOFA

COFFEE
TABLE

ARMCHAIR

TELEPHONE

SMALL
TABLE

PROSCENIUM

92

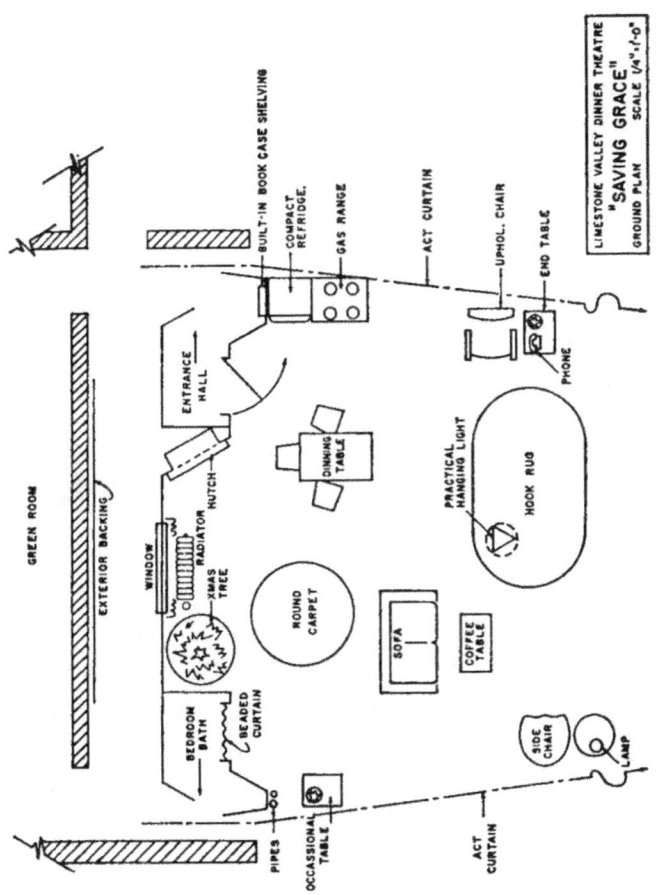

GREEN ROOM

EXTERIOR BACKING

WINDOW

XMAS TREE

RADIATOR

BEDROOM BATH

BEADED CURTAIN

PIPES

OCCASSIONAL TABLE

ACT CURTAIN

SIDE CHAIR

LAMP

SOFA

COFFEE TABLE

ROUND CARPET

DINING TABLE

HUTCH

ENTRANCE HALL

PRACTICAL HANGING LIGHT

HOOK RUG

BUILT-IN BOOK CASE SHELVING

COMPACT REFRIDGE.

GAS RANGE

ACT CURTAIN

UPHOL. CHAIR

END TABLE

PHONE

LIMESTONE VALLEY DINNER THEATRE
"SAVING GRACE"
GROUND PLAN   SCALE 1/4"-1'-0"

93

MUSIC USE NOTE

Licensees are solely responsible for obtaining formal written permission from copyright owners to use copyrighted music in the performance of this play and are strongly cautioned to do so. If no such permission is obtained by the licensee, then the licensee must use only original music that the licensee owns and controls. Licensees are solely responsible and liable for all music clearances and shall indemnify the copyright owners of the play(s) and their licensing agent, Samuel French, against any costs, expenses, losses and liabilities arising from the use of music by licensees. Please contact the appropriate music licensing authority in your territory for the rights to any incidental music.

IMPORTANT BILLING AND CREDIT REQUIREMENTS

If you have obtained performance rights to this title, please refer to your licensing agreement for important billing and credit requirements.

www.ingramcontent.com/pod-product-compliance
Lightning Source LLC
Chambersburg PA
CBHW070349120726
47909CB00008B/2772